Dragon Blood 4: Knight

Dragon Blood 4
Knight

Avril Sabine

Cracked Acorn Productions
Australia

Dragon Blood 4: Knight

Published by

Cracked Acorn Productions

PO Box 1365

Gympie, Queensland 4570

Australia

978-1-925131-30-7 (Kindle)

978-1-925617-65-8 (EPUB)

978-1-925131-41-3 (Print)

Genre: Young Adult Urban Fantasy

Copyright 2015 © Avril Sabine

Cover design by Caitlyn Petersen

Yep, still for the three of you.

Amber is starting to feel that her list of enemies is growing longer by the minute. Those she cares about are threatened and during a surprise attack she fears one of her people is killed. Her life is spinning out of control, there are too many people she desperately wants to keep safe, but she can't be with all of them at once. There's only one of her and so many of them. It's tearing her apart.

*

This story was written by an Australian author using Australian spelling.

Name Pronunciation

Like many names there is more than one way to pronounce the following ones. These are the pronunciations used in this series.

Names:

Alsandair (ahl-san-dare)

Anrai (arn-ree)

Bredon (bread-en)

Chait (single syllable, rhymes with hate)

Daray (dah-ray)

Doneele (donny-lee)

Emlyn (em-lin)

Gair (rhymes with hair)

Gethin (geh-thin)

Isleen (ish-lean)

Kiani (key-ah-knee)

Laren (lah-rin)

Maira (may-rah)

Orin (oh-rin)

Paili (pah-lee)

Queran (qwhere-rin)

Rhobert (row-bert)

Rian (ree-in)

Ronan (row-nen)

Tahmid (tar-mid)

Turi (two-ree)

Other pronunciations:

Erilan (era-len)

Feralenzi (fair-a-len-zee)

Pliethin (plea-thin)

Temolae (tem-oh-lay)

Chapter One

Amber checked the screen of her ringing phone, momentarily closing her eyes when she saw it was Cooper. She rejected the call and quickly sent a text. *Can't talk. Out to dinner with Mum.* She wasn't quite there yet, but they would be soon enough.

"Who was that?" Donna parked the car on the side of the road, out the front of a lowset, dark red, brick house.

"No one important," Amber muttered as she unbuckled and got out of the car. Although she'd much prefer to answer what was probably the twentieth call from Cooper than go to dinner with her mother. It was the worst way to end the school holidays. She didn't even know these people. Why would she want to have dinner with them?

Donna joined her on the footpath. "Don't start, Amber. I let you spend your entire holidays with those… those-” Donna broke off her sentence. “Well, the least you can do is be nice tonight.”

“Dragons. There’s nothing wrong with the word.”

“Please, Amber. I ask so little of you lately. One normal night. Is that too much to ask for?”

With the way things had been going lately, asking for the moon might have been a more realistic request. “Probably.”

“So you won’t even try.”

“I didn’t say that. I just said that a normal night was probably too much to ask for. I didn’t plan for all this to happen. It just did.”

Donna sighed. “I wish Gary could have come.”

“Mum-” she had no idea what to say. She could apologise, but she wasn’t sure what she’d be apologising for. “Come on, let’s get this over and done with. And don’t you dare organise another dinner with Wayne and Jennifer. If she wants friends she can find her own instead of letting her father choose them for her.”

“Just be nice.”

“Fine.” Amber followed her mother as they headed for the front door. She could probably dredge up nice from somewhere. Somewhere beyond battles, assassins and blood soaked dreams. Who was she kidding? She didn’t even know if nice was in her vocabulary any more. She thought of the last dragon she'd help kill. Queran. She hadn't even known his name at the time. Queran and Paili. How many did she have to kill before it became meaningless?

They reached the front door and Donna turned to Amber and whispered, "Be nice." She knocked on the door, stepping back to wait.

There was the sound of footsteps then Wayne swung open the door. Amber remembered him from the time they'd run into him while shopping. He still smelt strange under his excess of aftershave. Like last time, he wore a t-shirt and jeans, muscular arms making the band of his sleeves look tight. His sandy brown hair was still little more than stubble.

Wayne smiled. "I'm glad you could make it. No problem following the directions I gave you?" He looked past them. "Weren't you bringing your boyfriend?"

"A last minute call from a patient. I'm afraid he won't be able to make it," Donna said.

"Maybe next time." Wayne's smile stayed in place. "Come in. Come and meet my daughter." He gestured inside with a wave of his hand. "She's nearly finished setting the table."

Amber trailed behind them, her gaze darting everywhere. When she found herself looking for escape routes and vantage points, she immediately stopped. It was a dinner. Not a battle. She had to stop expecting something to jump out from the shadows all the time. Nothing was going to get her. Besides, Chait was still guarding her from the Void so it wasn't like she was unprotected. He wouldn't be game to let anything happen to her. Ronan would hunt him down and rip out his heart if he failed to protect her.

They stepped into a dining room. Wayne, still smiling, gestured towards the girl placing cutlery on the table. "This is my daughter Jennifer."

"Hi." The girl had the same smile and sandy blond hair as her father. It was cut longer than his, but not by much.

"Hi." The smile made Amber feel nervous. Or maybe it was the strange scent that both father and daughter had. She still couldn't place it even though she was certain she'd smelt it before.

Donna moved forward, smiling. "I'm so glad to finally meet you. Your father has told me so much about you."

"I hope it was good." Jennifer laughed.

Amber barely managed not to wince at how fake the laugh sounded. Maybe the girl was nervous. Or maybe she was finding fault where there was none because she didn't want to be here. And what could she say to get the meal started so they could get the night over and done with? Everything she thought of sounded rude and she was supposed to be nice tonight. Somehow.

"Take a seat." Wayne pulled a chair out from the table, his smile widening as he gestured for Donna to sit at the head of the table. "Place of honour for our guest."

Amber resisted the urge to gag. Could the pair of them be more pathetic? She quickly sat in a chair near her mother to avoid Wayne needing to continue with his theatrics. It was a waste of effort.

"Sweetheart, get the food from the kitchen." He turned away from his daughter. "You wait until you taste the food Jennifer cooked for you." He kissed his fingers theatrically. "Bellissimo."

"I can't wait. What did she cook?" Donna asked.

"Here it is now." Wayne nodded towards Jennifer as she walked back into the room with two plates. "Roast beef and vegetables with a rich gravy she made from scratch using the pan juices."

Jennifer put a plate in front of Donna and Amber, still smiling as she headed out of the room.

"Eat up." Wayne continued to stand.

"Oh no, we'll wait until everyone is served," Donna said.

Amber leaned forward to breathe in the smell of the food. It smelt odd. Like Wayne and Jennifer. Where had she smelt this scent before? Then it hit her. At her grandmother's home. As Jennifer placed two more plates on the table, Amber leapt from her seat, dragging Donna away from the table. "Dragon bone."

"Amber!" Donna looked shocked.

"Don't eat it," Amber said. "There's dragon bone in it."

"I'm sorry–" Donna started to say, breaking off at the look on Wayne's face.

"They said you didn't know," Wayne said.

"What?" Donna looked from Wayne to Jennifer. She took a step backwards.

Amber saw Chait appear out of the Void behind Wayne and his daughter. *"Not yet. Wait and see what's going on."* He nodded and disappeared back into the Void, but Amber felt safer knowing he was ready to help.

Wayne's gaze remained on Amber. "But even if you did know, there's no way you could have known there was dragon bone in the gravy. It's too strong a scent for anyone except a dragon to be able to smell the bone through it."

"I'm not a dragon," Amber said.

"Then what are you?" Wayne demanded.

"What's going on?" Donna asked.

"What are you?" Amber held Wayne's gaze while keeping track of Jennifer's movements. She pointed a finger in Jennifer's direction. "Don't move until someone answers. Although I think I've got a pretty good idea."

"Knights."

Amber nodded at Wayne's reply, ignoring her mother's gasp. "Why us?"

"We need Helen to come back. If her daughter and granddaughter join us we're certain she'll return," Wayne said.

Amber sent a look to Jennifer. "I'm serious. Don't move."

"But we already answered you." Jennifer took another step in their direction.

"One more step towards us and we're out of here," Amber warned.

Wayne waved Jennifer back. "You don't know what you're missing. The calling that should have been yours if Helen hadn't quit. You've missed out on so much."

"I know what I'm missing and I'm not interested," Amber said.

"This was all about getting to my mother?" Donna asked.

Wayne shook his head. "Not quite. It was about convincing her to return to the world she was born for."

"This was all about my mother?" Donna's voice rose slightly.

"No-"

Amber interrupted Wayne. "Why the dragon bone in our food?"

"To show you how much better life can be with it. It makes you stronger, healthier, live longer. If you join the Knights you could have it regularly," Wayne said.

Was that what it was really about? Not just killing dragons, but living longer. "Why do you kill dragons?"

"If you knew dragons like we did you wouldn't be asking that question. They hate people and kill them for no reason at all. You've been brainwashed by movies and books into thinking they're wonderful," Wayne said.

"They're vicious, murderous creatures," Jennifer said.

"But-"

Amber cut off her mother's words before she said

something to contradict them. "Are Wayne and Jennifer Smith really your names?"

Wayne smiled. "Almost. Our surname is Naylor."

Amber hated that smile. It reminded her of a used car salesman and she wasn't interested in buying anything he had to sell. "I think it's time we left."

"Try it. Just try a bit." Wayne gestured towards the table.

Amber shook her head, taking a step backwards. "Come on, Mum." She reached for Donna's arm.

"If you tried some you'd understand what we're talking about." Wayne stepped around the table, slowly advancing on them. "It doesn't hurt, I swear."

"It's the bones of people," Donna said.

"They aren't really people. They might be able to turn into people, but they're animals," Wayne said.

"Vicious beasts." Jennifer advanced on them from around the other side of the table.

Chait appeared in the room, tackling Wayne. "Behind you."

Amber spun to see an athletic looking, blond woman, her hair cut in a similar style to Jennifer's.

"You!" Donna pointed an accusing finger at the woman.

"Let me go." Wayne struggled to escape Chait. Jennifer threw herself on them.

"Who is she?" Amber demanded after checking that Chait could cope with the two Knights.

The woman held out a hand. "I'm Vikki."

Amber didn't take the offered hand, particularly since the woman's smile reminded her of Wayne's slick one.

The woman dropped her hand. "Vikki Naylor."

Amber frowned. "Wayne's wife?"

Vikki laughed. "His sister."

Amber looked towards her mother, who gripped her arm tightly. "Mum?"

"It's the woman your father's been seeing."

Amber stared at the woman in horror.

Vikki's smile vanished. "Oh no, it wasn't anything like that. I mean," she gave a little laugh, "how could I help myself? I was only supposed to approach you Donna, but well," she shrugged her shoulders, "one thing led to another."

"You're the woman my dad's been seeing?" Amber couldn't believe he'd chosen this fake woman over her mother.

"Vikki! Get this man off me," Wayne bellowed.

"Surely the two of you can deal with a single man." Vikki barely gave them a glance. "Incompetent."

Amber's phone rang and she pulled it out to see it was Cooper. "Not now!" She hung up. How had this night gone so crazy so quickly? Wayne was a Knight? Her father was dating a Knight? She shook her head. It was meant to be a simple dinner. An occasion that should have had her bored out of her mind, not warily waiting to be attacked. "We have to go."

Vikki smiled. "Oh no you don't. I believe you have yet to try the meal my niece spent all afternoon preparing."

"No thank you. I'm not hungry." Amber's phone rang again and she saw it was Cooper. "What?"

"I really need to talk to you."

"Not now, Cooper. I've got a situation I need to deal with first."

"They found me, Amber. They're out the front of the unit. They're telling me that if I come quietly they won't hurt me."

Amber swore. "Give me a minute." She hung up on him, dialling Ronan's number. Her first thought had been to call Kade, but Ronan knew the pathways through the Void better than anyone. She blinked when Vikki pulled out a gun. "Ronan. Problems."

"Hang up, now," Vikki ordered.

"What's up, kitten?" Ronan asked.

"Save Cooper, then I need you."

"This better be good." Ronan disconnected.

Amber returned her phone to her pocket. "Look, Vikki, I suggest letting us go before all hell breaks loose." She didn't know if she could disarm the woman before she could get off a shot. And she wasn't about to risk it while her mother was standing beside her going to pieces. Half the words Donna muttered were unintelligible and the other half Amber wished were. "We're not going to die, Mum."

"Vikki if you don't deal with this man I swear I'll get even," Wayne yelled.

"What do you want me to do? Shoot him?" Vikki demanded.

"Don't be stupid. You might hit Jennifer or me."

"This is your last chance," Amber warned.

"Or what?" Vikki asked smugly. "In case you hadn't noticed, I've got a gun and I will use it if you don't eat the food."

"Grandma isn't about to return to the Knights if you kill us," Amber said.

"Oh I wouldn't kill you, just hurt you a tiny bit." Vikki's smile widened.

"Vikki!" Wayne bellowed.

"Try and not be so incompetent, Wayne." Vikki didn't even look in his direction. "Now you two go eat."

Amber stepped in front of her mother. She could heal herself, she couldn't heal her mother. "No."

Vikki lowered the gun, pointing it at Amber's leg. "I'll give you to the count of ten."

Ronan stepped out of the Void. "I'll give you to the count of three." He smiled, his predatory one.

Amber wanted to throw herself at him and thank him for coming. "What took you so long?"

"A dragon." Vikki turned the gun towards Ronan.

"I had to knock your boy out. He was hysterical." Ronan battered the gun out of Vikki's hand and she threw herself towards it. *"And I had to walk some of the Void to get in the right place. Maybe in future you should let me learn the pathways of wherever you're planning to go. Might make things easier."* He grabbed Vikki around the waist before she could reach the gun.

Chait moved to Amber's side.

"What happened to Wayne?" She turned around to see two crumpled bodies. "And Jennifer."

"They're alive," Chait said.

Vikki struggled in Ronan's arms. "Traitors. You'll never be Knights if you've sided with the dragons."

"You were the ones who brought us here. Not the other way around." Amber turned to her mother. "Mum! Stop! We're not going to die."

"We're leaving this town," Donna said.

"No, we're not." She turned back to Vikki. "I've already agreed to my grandparent's request to give the Knights a chance."

Vikki stilled. "Grandparents? Charles? You've spoken to Charles?"

Amber nodded.

"He's coming back?"

Amber was surprised by the amount of awe in Vikki's voice. You'd think she was talking about her favourite movie star. "Yes."

"When?"

"I don't know."

"Negotiations are ongoing," Ronan said.

Amber nearly smiled. That was a mild word for the arguments.

"These are the dragons you're negotiating with for his release?"

"I thought he-" Donna started to say.

Amber rounded on her mother. "Mum!" She didn't want the Knights to know all their business. She turned back to Vikki. "We're going."

"What about the dragon bone?" Vikki's gaze was drawn towards the table.

"You eat it. I'm not interested." Grabbing her mother's arm, Amber strode towards the front door.

"You could almost live forever if you had enough," Vikki called after them.

Amber kept walking, glad to reach the car. "You want me to drive?"

Donna handed over the keys, slumping into the passenger seat.

"I'll talk to you later, kitten." Ronan left through the Void before Amber could reply.

She stared down at her mother for a moment before she closed the door Donna had left open. She was going to be in so much trouble when her mother finally found out that she'd let her grandparents be imprisoned. And she doubted very much that her grandparents would be kind enough to keep that information to themselves. Walking around the front of the car, she slid into the driver's seat and started the engine.

She'd been right. It had been a terrible end to the school holidays. She thought of Cooper. And the fun obviously wasn't over. She only hoped that Ronan's threat of talking to her later would occur much later. Maybe even days later. But she didn't hold out much hope for that.

Chapter Two

Amber clambered into the backseat of Maira's car, relieved school was over for the day. Lately she'd been wondering why she even bothered with it. After arriving back at Kade's place last night she'd had to spend hours calming Cooper down. Ronan had dumped him in the lounge room and he'd regained consciousness not long after she'd arrived home. She rested her head on Kade's shoulder when he got in the back seat with her, Brann getting in the front passenger seat.

Maira started the car once all the doors were closed. "Straight home, Kade?"

"That answer better be a yes," Amber warned.

Kade smiled. "Yeah."

She momentarily closed her eyes, yawning. "Actually, on second thought maybe we should just keep driving. Cooper sent me a million texts today and he's sure to pounce on me the moment we get home."

"I'll deal with him," Kade said.

"You scare him."

"Everything scares him," Kade said. "Even you sometimes."

"Obviously not enough or he wouldn't be texting and ringing me every other minute, expecting me to tell him what to do. Why would I care if he wears a green shirt or a red one?"

"Tell him the red one will hide fresh blood better," Kade said.

Amber chuckled. "I doubt that comment would help." She fell silent, drifting off to sleep to be woken by the car stopping, biting back a groan when she saw Cooper burst out of the house. He stopped mid stride when Ronan appeared out of the Void. "Now what?" She slowly got out of the car, walking towards Ronan, trying to gauge his mood.

Ronan's gaze brushed past Amber before he met her eyes. "You need to talk to your grandparents."

"Why?"

"Do you have to question everything?"

Okay, so maybe his mood wasn't much better than hers. She turned to Kade, giving him her schoolbag. "I'll be back later." She sent a look towards Cooper who was frozen on the verandah, a terrified expression on his face. "Take care of Cooper for me." She leaned forward, brushing her lips across Kade's, her hand resting on his chest.

"Now, Amber." Ronan's voice was sharp.

She grinned. "Try not to kill him. I know he's annoying, but-" she shrugged, turning to Ronan. "Okay." Drawing the word out, she didn't have a chance to say anything else. Ronan grabbed her arm, tugged her away from Kade, and took her to his house through the Void. They arrived at his rooftop water garden. She pulled away from him. "What's going on? Why here?" Last time he'd brought her to this spot it had been to grill her. She wasn't hiding any secrets from him so what bad news did he have for her this time?

"Your grandparents have offered to hold their peace until the first of next year and not to hunt any of your dragons until after that time. Their wording, not mine."

Amber grinned. "My dragons, huh?"

"Don't be smart, Amber."

"Can we trust them to keep their word?"

"I'll have them watched."

She stared at him, trying to figure out his angle.

He never did anything for anyone unless it benefited him. "Why?"

"I thought you wanted this."

"Nice try. Why?"

"You gave them a month of your time. It can't start until they're free."

"Come on, Ronan. I know you never do anything out of the goodness of your heart. I'd be surprised if there actually was any goodness left in it."

Ronan smiled. "Very good. You're learning. No dragon does anything unless it benefits them. Don't you forget that."

"What do you want, Ronan?" She didn't even bother to keep the irritation from her voice. There was no point hiding what he could probably see anyway.

"You at my side when I take down the Elder."

She backed away, holding up a hand. "Oh no. Definitely not."

Ronan grabbed her hand, stopping her retreat. "He wants you dead."

She tried to tug her hand from his grip but he wouldn't let her go. "You can kill him without my help."

"He tried to kill your people, don't you want to personally take care of him?"

"No. He failed."

Ronan tugged her closer, a flash of gold appearing in his eyes. "Once I hand on the proof, things will happen fast. It must be us that take him out. We're the ones he was after, we have to show strength to all the others who'd climb over us to get the Council position."

"I've been in too many battles." Again she tried to pull away. "I can't keep killing people. No more, Ronan." Her voice dropped, weariness entering it. "No more. Please."

"You're a Dragon Mage. Show weakness and you're dead. You and all your people. Is that what you want, Amber?"

She glared at him. Obviously she was tired if she thought Ronan would show her any mercy.

"Take me to my grandparents."

"One month, then we take down Tahmid. You and I together."

"Who?"

"The Elder."

She continued to hold his gaze, trying to figure out if he told the truth. Yeah, he probably did. He looked far too certain of the outcome.

"You owe me two favours, Amber. And probably one for the help I gave you last night."

So he'd been trying to get out of using them. Typical. "Fine. Take me to my grandparents."

"One month."

"Maybe. We'll see what happens during the next month." Hopefully nothing, but she wasn't counting on it. Not with her current luck.

"As soon as possible after the month is up."

She hesitated a moment longer before she nodded. "Now take me to my grandparents."

Ronan tightened his grip, taking her through the Void to the door keeping Helen and Charles imprisoned. Letting Amber go, he unlocked the door and after checking inside, waved her in.

What was he doing? She stepped inside, turning to face the door that closed, hearing Ronan lock it. Even though she knew better, she still tried to mentally reach outside the room. As expected, she failed to contact Ronan. Nothing about the room had changed since she'd last been in it. Great. She was locked in a room, alone with her grandparents. Maybe Ronan didn't really need her and actually wanted her dead.

"About time you got here," Charles said. "We told him to bring you this morning."

Amber slowly turned to face the room and her

grandparents. They didn't look like they were out for her blood. Yet. "I had school."

"Did he explain our terms to you?" Helen asked.

"You can't expect a dragon to explain things correctly. He's sure to have changed some things to suit himself. Or left things out." Charles gestured towards the dining suite. "Sit down."

She stared at him for a moment before she walked towards the table and pulled out a chair. Standing beside the chair, she waited. "Aren't you joining me?"

Helen sat down.

Amber continued to watch Charles until he sat at the table too. She finally sat on a chair. "He said you want me to start my month with the Knights."

"He said they tried to make you eat dragon bone. At gunpoint," Charles said.

She nodded. "Yeah. Vikki Naylor was going to shoot Mum." She hoped that would make a difference to them. The only one of their descendants that was still human.

Charles turned to his wife. "I wonder if she's Wallace Naylor's daughter."

"It wouldn't surprise me. He always was a bit of an extremist."

Obviously a threat to their daughter wasn't enough to upset them. Maybe a different tactic would work.

"She did it to force you to come back to them, Grandma."

"As if I'd let her force me to rejoin the Knights if I chose not to," Helen said.

Amber bit back the angry words that threatened to spill. Didn't they care about anyone else in their family? "What are your terms?"

"We're returning to Brisbane and the Knights' headquarters and–"

Amber interrupted Charles. "No."

"What do you mean no?"

"I didn't know I'd have to go to Brisbane."

"You're the most contrary child imaginable. You've spent months moping and complaining that you wanted to go home and now you can, you refuse to go. You were the one who agreed to give the Knights a month to prove themselves. What was all the whinging Donna and I had to put up with about you wanting to go home?"

"It wasn't months. It was only days. And things have changed. I can't move until the end of the year." Kade had to remain in the same town for a year. That wasn't up until the last day of the year. Nearly three months away.

"You agreed to spend time with the Knights," Helen said.

"On the weekends," Amber suggested.

"Eight days is nothing like thirty-one. No deal," Charles said.

"Friday afternoon until Monday morning. That's as good as three days," Amber said.

"That's twelve days at the most. I'll accept that if you do thirty-one days three days at a time."

Amber shook her head. "No way. I hadn't planned to be with the Knights every single day anyway. I don't even spend every second of my days with the dragons." Well, some days she did, but that wouldn't help her argument. "Besides, I've got Topaz the last week of this month and the first week of November."

"You're as bad as a dragon." Helen glared at her. "It's hard to believe we're related."

Amber refused to look away from Helen's gaze. "I've always said that. Glad to see someone's finally listened and agreed."

Charles pointed a finger at her. "You will apologise to your grandmother immediately. I won't have you talking to her like that."

"She started it."

"Apologise," Charles snapped.

Amber rose to her feet. "I'm wasting my time. You're trying to get more from the deal than you're entitled to."

Charles also rose. "You're the one trying to get out of the bargain you made."

"What did you expect me to do? Live with the Knights for an entire month?"

"Yes!"

"You what?"

"You heard me."

Amber shook her head, certain she must have been mistaken. Surely her grandfather hadn't said she had to live with the Knights. "I have school."

"Knights are homeschooled. It takes more than a typical education to survive as a Knight," Helen said.

"I have seven weeks left of school."

"We'll wait until then," Charles said.

Amber didn't think Ronan would be happy with that plan. She withdrew her phone and sent him a text. *They want me to live with the Knights for an entire month.*

Ronan entered the room, slamming the door shut behind him.

Helen jumped to her feet, sending a glare Amber's way. "You called him in here. Traitor!"

"You're trying to change the terms of the deal," Ronan said.

"She's trying to get out of the deal." Charles pointed a finger in Amber's direction.

"I'm not. They're the ones trying to get more from this than they're supposed to."

"He isn't part of these negotiations," Charles said.

Amber opened her mouth, but Ronan spoke before she could.

"I hold you prisoner. Not Amber. You're in my care. I was the one who managed the negotiations and I still have a claim on some of Amber's time."

"The negotiations were made with something Amber owned," Charles said.

"She didn't know the value of what she owned. I helped her get a price she was happy with for the object," Ronan said.

Amber slammed her hands down on the table. "Stop. It's simple. I won't move in with the Knights. It's not happening. I never agreed to it. It was never even implied. I'll give them a month. They can have most of my afternoons and from Friday afternoon until Monday morning. That's it. Nothing more."

The negotiations continued, each side arguing the other was ripping them off. Eventually, an agreement was reached. Amber would spend time with the Knights, giving them three afternoons as well as from Friday afternoon to Monday morning. It would start that weekend and last for six weekends, ending the week before school finished. Amber just hoped that gave her enough time to study for exam week.

Amber paused at the door, turning back to her grandparents. "Don't forget you're not to tell Mum you were imprisoned here."

"As if I'd want anyone to know my own granddaughter had done that to us." Helen almost spat the words at her.

"I'll see you Friday." She slipped out the door, waiting for Ronan to join her, locking the door behind himself. "Can you take me home now?"

"Why did you call me to negotiate for you?"

"Because I knew you could get a better deal than I could."

Ronan smiled. "So you owe me a favour."

She wasn't about to owe him another favour when it looked like she'd soon be out of his debt. "No. It was only because you had a claim on my time once the Knights were finished with me and I knew you wouldn't want to wait any longer than you had to." She grinned when he glared at her for throwing his words back at him.

"You expect me to believe it was for my benefit."

"Of course it was. Hadn't you not long finished telling me you were letting them go early because you wanted me to finish up with them sooner?"

Ronan didn't bother answering. He grabbed her arm and took her through the Void, leaving her on Kade's doorstep before he disappeared. Amber grinned, deciding to take that as a victory against Ronan. She planned to enjoy it since it was probably an extremely rare occurrence.

"Amber?"

Her smile disappeared as Cooper opened the front door. So much for enjoying it. "What?"

"Are you coming inside?" His gaze searched the area "Has Ronan gone already?"

"Yeah." She pushed past him to step into the lounge room. The sooner she finished with the Knights the sooner she could remove the threat from Cooper's life so he could get out of hers. She ignored the little voice that told her that getting rid of two problems wouldn't stop others from forming.

Chapter Three

After a week of putting up with Cooper underfoot, Amber was almost relieved to go to the Knights for the weekend. She slung her bag over one shoulder, several changes of clothes and her phone charger packed in it. Her gaze met Kade's. "I'm ready."

"Call me if you have the slightest problem," Kade said.

"You don't have to tell me a million times." Her gaze momentarily fell on Cooper huddled in one of the faded floral armchairs in Kade's lounge room. Kade hadn't been the only one who'd been repetitive. Cooper had kept asking her why she had to go. "Everything will be fine and I'll see you Monday morning."

Kade nodded, reaching for her. He took her through the void to the shadows under a large fig tree at the front of the Knights' headquarters that Ronan had shown him the pathway to. Before he let her go, Kade kissed her, his arms tightening around her.

She clung to him, not wanting to let go. Monday seemed an eternity away. "I'll be fine. Chait will keep an eye on me from the Void." She slowly drew away from him. "You're the one that needs to be careful. Tahmid is still looking for Cooper and he won't care who gets in the way."

"I can take care of myself."

"You better." She stepped forward to kiss him one last time before she spun and hurried to the front door of the Knights' headquarters. The door swung open before she had a chance to raise her hand and knock.

A boy around her age grinned at her, white blond hair falling in his blue eyes. "I'm Dominic. Our grandfathers were brothers."

"Were?" Amber tried not to wrinkle her nose at the smell of dragon bone. Did every Knight take it?

"Mine died years ago.

"Oh, sorry."

"So anyway, I guess we're cousins of sorts."

"Cousins." She couldn't help thinking about her cousin Shylah and her father. Roger was still having problems being released from his promise not to contact his human family.

"Yep." Dominic held the door open further.

"Anyway, I've been asked to take you to the conference room the moment you arrive."

"Okay." She stepped inside, her gaze darting around. The walls were white and bare, the floor tiled. The room had a counter that made it look like a reception area and behind that was another closed door. It reminded her of an office entrance. It looked far too innocent and ordinary to be the Brisbane headquarters of the Knights.

She followed Dominic to the door behind the counter. He opened it and waved her through. Before Amber had a chance to move, her phone rang. Pulling it out, she was surprised to see it was Ronan. "Yeah?"

"Chait can't follow you into the Knights' headquarters. What they've built it from prevents people from remaining in the Void."

"What am I supposed to do?"

"Be careful."

"That's not very helpful."

"You don't have a choice, Amber. You made the deal, you can't go back on it now. Just be careful."

"Okay." She stared at her phone when Ronan disconnected. Should she ring Kade? No, absolutely not. He'd probably demand she leave, and she couldn't. As Ronan had pointed out, she'd made the deal. She returned her phone to her pocket. "Sorry."

Dominic nodded. "That's okay. Follow me." He led the way along the corridor, entering a room at the end. "Wait here." Closing the door behind him, he left her alone in the room.

Amber looked around. A large table, surrounded by chairs, dominated the room and kind of reminded her of the planning room in her castle, Temolae Keep. She remained standing, keeping an eye on the door. Her grandfather was the first to arrive, closely followed by a man he introduced as Martin. He had pale blond hair, slightly yellowed, and sharp blue eyes that reminded her of her grandfather's. Particularly with how they eyed her up and down like some specimen under a microscope.

"Your grandfather tells me you've spent a lot of time with dragons lately."

Amber nodded, shooting Charles a glare. Was this how he kept his word? She took a deep breath, her gaze returning to her grandfather. He was taking dragon bone too. It wasn't just Martin. The scent was too strong for it to be only one of them.

"Where did they take you?"

Her gaze was drawn back to Martin. "Dragon lands."

"No. Where did they take you in our world?"

Again she looked at Charles. He stood with his arms crossed, staring at her, a look of what might be victory on his face. Two could play this game. She hadn't spent months with dragons without learning something. She crossed her own arms over her chest as she met Martin's gaze. "Have you ever been through the Void?"

"Of course I haven't," Martin said. "Only dragons can travel through the Void."

"You might know where you started, but unless you've been to the place before, you won't know where you've ended up."

"So you're saying you don't know where they took you."

She shrugged, trying not to smile. One of Ronan's predatory smiles would have been just perfect for the occasion. "I can't help you. Sorry." She probably should have put in a bit more effort to actually make her tone sound sorry, but she was too angry. How dare they grill her the moment she entered their building. This better not be how the rest of the weekend went. She hadn't agreed to an interrogation.

"And you have no clue at all, of where you were taken."

Again she shrugged. "Every house looks pretty

similar from the inside. You can't always tell a location from standing inside a room." She gestured to the room they stood in. "Even this one. We could be anywhere. Even France."

Charles' gaze narrowed. "Are you sure there isn't anything you want to tell Martin?"

She met her grandfather's sharp blue eyes, refusing to give in to the demands she saw in them. "Not a single thing, but I do have questions of my own. Like where do I sleep this weekend?" Her gaze travelled to Martin. "I need somewhere to put my bag."

"We don't tolerate impertinence around here." Martin's gaze remained on her as he let silence fill the room. "I'll send Dominic to take you to your room." With one last hard look, he stalked out, letting the door close behind him.

Charles pointed a finger at her. "Don't think you'll be able to keep getting away with protecting them."

"Why are you eating dragon bone?"

"Don't interrupt. Come the first of the year, they're all dead. We'll hunt them down and kill them." He spun on his heel, striding from the room, slamming the door behind him.

Great. She was now looking forward to getting to know the Knights even less. She thought over her agreement and couldn't think of any way to get out of it. Next time she made an agreement like this she'd also add in how they were to treat her.

The door swung open and Dominic stood there, smiling. "Glad to see I'm not the only one who pisses off my old man. You coming?" He held the door open wider. When Amber joined him, he headed down the corridor. "So what did you say to him?"

Martin was his father? Charles' nephew? It shouldn't have surprised her at all. "Nothing." And that had been the problem since he'd wanted her to tell him her secrets. There was no way she was going to endanger any of her people. They were going to have to do better than that if they wanted to get any information out of her. She thought of Daray, the dragon Ronan had tortured. Hopefully the Knights weren't willing to go that far.

Dominic sent her a look of disbelief. "Really? Not a single word?"

Amber shrugged. "I just tend to have that effect on people."

"It might be worth saying more than nothing next time. You don't want him taking privileges off you."

Amber shrugged, keeping pace with Dominic. He led her through numerous corridors that all looked the same, passing closed doors at regular intervals. White tiles, white walls, fluorescent lighting. A sterile and featureless environment. He opened a door partway along a corridor, gesturing for her to enter.

Amber continued to stand in the doorway, looking into the room. A single metal framed bed was against one wall, a narrow window with a closed blind that hung within the window frame filled part of the wall behind the bed. The entrance to the room felt like a hallway due to the built-in wardrobe that jutted into the room to the right of the door.

"I'll be back for you in about half an hour. Give you time to put your gear away," Dominic said.

Stepping into the room, Amber dropped her bag on the floor in front of the wardrobe. "Done."

"I wouldn't do that if I was you. They get pretty upset around here if you leave your room in a mess."

"You're kidding, right?" He considered that a mess? He really didn't want to see her bedroom at home then.

Dominic shook his head. "Not at all. I'll be back after you've unpacked."

"Don't bother leaving." She slid open the wardrobe door, kicked her bag in and closed the door. "Done." She met Dominic's gaze, daring him to disagree with her. She wasn't about to unpack. There was no way she was making herself that comfortable. As soon as Monday morning arrived she was out of here.

"Are you sure you want to do that?"

"Yes."

Dominic stared at her a moment longer before he shrugged. "Come on then." He led her through several more corridors, stopping in a room with about twenty kids. "Rec room."

Remaining by the door, Amber glanced around. There were several couches placed in front of a television at one end. Some kids were sitting in them, but there were more sprawled on the ground, using large cushions. At the other end was a kitchenette, three kids standing around talking. "How many families live here?"

"None. During school term it's like a boarding school."

"But some of those kids look really young." Amber eyed two of the kids sitting on cushions.

"Nah, they've been here a couple of years now. The youngest we've got at the moment is eight."

"Eight."

Dominic nodded. "Yeah."

"What age do you start here?"

"Six."

"Six?"

"Yes, six. Do you have to repeat everything I say?"

Amber shook her head, trying to imagine what

it'd be like to leave home at six. "Don't they get homesick?"

"Knights do not succumb to weaknesses like that."

She didn't know what to say. Her grandmother telling her daughter not to be weak and cry came to mind. Maybe there was no difference between the Knights and dragons. Other than one had the ability to shift out of human form. "So what do you do around here for fun?"

"We learn to kill dragons."

"No, I mean after classes or whatever you call them."

"Killing dragons is fun."

She felt like rolling her eyes. Was he being deliberately annoying? "What do you do when you're taking a break from learning to be a Knight?"

"We never take a break from being Knights. We're always Knights."

"But surely you do other stuff."

"We're here to learn to be Knights. Isn't that why you're here? To learn how to become a Knight and fight dragons."

'Not exactly' didn't seem like the right thing to say to Dominic. Not when he had an expression that clearly said any answer other than yes wouldn't be acceptable. Unless it was, hell yeah. "They didn't tell me what to expect."

Dominic grinned. "No wonder you're so confused. You're going to love it here. In our weekend classes we learn different styles of fighting. All the mainstream classes are during the week until two p.m. and then we have more fighting classes every afternoon until six." He gestured towards the kids in front of the television. "We've not long finished for the day."

"Why weren't you in your fighting class when I arrived earlier?"

"I had permission to leave the class early to greet you."

She almost felt like she should apologise. "Oh."

"But that's all right. It was just a practice session."

"Okay."

"So did you want to watch some television before we go in to dinner?"

She really didn't feel like meeting anyone else and if she joined the group in front of the television, they'd probably expect an introduction. "What else is there to do?"

"I could show you the library and you could pick out a book to read in your room."

"Uhm, okay." Anything had to be better than

sitting amongst a group of kids she didn't know and had nothing in common with. Killing dragons wasn't fun. She thought of Paili and Queran. Not in the least like fun.

"This way." Dominic led her down more corridors, pushing open the door of a large, book lined room. Bookcases took up every wall and there were several rows down the centre of the room. He gestured inside. "Help yourself."

Chapter Four

When Amber entered the room and started looking through the books, she found they were all about killing dragons and fighting techniques. She flicked through one of the books that talked about dragon anatomy and where they were most vulnerable. Maybe it'd help her be a better healer.

"That's a really good book," Dominic said.

"Thanks." What else could she say? *I hope you never get the chance to use the information in it?* Like that'd go down well.

"I'll show you back to your room and draw you a map of how to find the rec room and dining room from there."

"Okay." Walking beside Dominic she tried to remember the way, but the corridors were all so featureless. She wracked her brain, trying to think of something to say, but couldn't come up with a single word. What did you talk about with someone who thought killing dragons was fun? There was no way she wanted to relive past kills.

When they reached her room, Dominic took a notebook and pen from his pocket and drew her two very basic maps. "Think you can follow them?"

She nodded. Hopefully.

"Make sure you're in the dining room by seven-thirty. If you're late you won't get dinner. The kitchenette in the rec room only has tea and coffee makings in it so don't go thinking you'll be able to get something to eat there."

"Okay."

"I'll see you at dinner then." With a quick grin, Dominic headed back along the corridor.

Amber stared after him, wondering how she was going to get through six weeks of this. Maybe she could hole up in her room and read. Although with the way things had been going for her lately, she'd still somehow fall into some sort of disaster. Closing the door behind her, she crossed the room and dropped onto the bed, folding the pillow before lying back on it. When she next checked the time, she saw she only had eight minutes to find the dining room.

Placing the book on the floor, open and face down so as to not lose her page, she checked the map before she hurried down the corridor. Trying the door that should have been the dining room, she found it was locked. She looked at the map again. Surely this was the right place. Pressing her ear against the door, she tried to hear if anything was happening inside. It wasn't seven-thirty yet, so why was the door locked?

There was a low murmur of voices and she strained her ears to hear what was happening. Was that her grandfather in there? Who was he talking to? It took her a moment to figure it out. Martin!

"Don't tell me that. I know. I've spent four decades as their prisoner, how could I not know?"

"Then make her cooperate."

"Easier said than done. She doesn't need us. She's made treaties with dragons to protect herself. We have to show her she's wrong. That all dragons must die."

"Then you should help us."

"I will. First of next year."

Fear skittered through Amber at her grandfather's words. She wasn't about to let him kill any of her dragons.

"That's too far away. Nearly three months. Why are you bothering to protect them? They wouldn't keep their word to us."

"Because we're better than them. We're Knights. Our word is our honour."

"There's nothing honourable about making deals with dragons."

"Do not speak to me like that." Charles' tone was cold. "I once held your position."

"Is that a threat?"

"No. It's a reminder."

"Then you should be willing to help us track down the dragons who held you."

"The only way you'll find them, before the start of the New Year, is by getting the information out of Amber."

Footsteps echoed down the corridor and Amber drew herself away from the door. No one was in sight yet, but she didn't want to be caught eavesdropping at the door no matter how badly she wanted to hear the rest of the conversation. She hurried back in the direction she'd come, glad it was away from the sound of footsteps. When she found her room, she dropped onto her bed.

It sounded like there was no way her grandfather would ever accept dragons in her life. She didn't know for certain about her grandmother, but if she had to take a guess, then she'd say she probably wouldn't either. It looked like one day soon she was going to have to choose sides. And she had family on both sides.

Dropping her head into her hands, she tried to think about what to do. It was impossible. There was nothing she could do. Rising to her feet, she pulled the blind open and stared out the barred window. The sound of traffic could be heard on a nearby road and she looked out onto the backyards of normal house blocks. Did all the rooms have bars, or had they been put on hers by order of her grandparents? It wasn't like she'd wanted to keep them imprisoned. She just hadn't known what else to do.

Her phone beeped a message and she checked it, groaning. It was from Cooper. *We haven't heard from you. Are you okay?* She shook her head, surprised he'd managed to go so many hours without texting her. She hoped Kade hadn't used Ronan's method of dealing with Cooper and knocked him out.

She typed in, *I'm fine.* Staring at the words for several minutes didn't help her think of anything else to say so she sent them.

Why didn't you let us know?

Should she reply or would that encourage him? Although he didn't really need any encouragement if the past week was anything to go by. *Quit messaging me. I'm busy.* When several minutes passed without another text, she returned her phone to her pocket. Her last text hadn't been a complete lie. She was busy. Thinking could be classed as being busy, especially when you had as many problems as she did.

The sound of the door opening had her spinning to face it, fireballs automatically filling her hands. She quickly extinguished them when she saw Dominic, open mouthed, in the doorway. Obviously not the best move. "Did you want something?"

He continued to stand there, his mouth still open.

"Dominic?" She took a step forwards.

He took half a step backwards. "Do they know?"

"Do who know what?"

"The High Protector. Your grandparents. Do they know you're a Dragon Mage?"

As usual, her luck was holding up just great. Bad luck that was. "My grandparents do, so I guess they've told the High Protector." Why did Dominic have to know about Dragon Mages?

"Would you have-" he gestured to her hands. "You know. Thrown them at me."

She shook her head. "You surprised me."

He looked disbelievingly at her. "Most people jump, not attack, when they're surprised."

"Most people haven't had an assassin after them," Amber said dryly.

"An assassin." He spoke it like it was a good thing. Reverently and with a touch of awe.

"Yes." Maybe she shouldn't have mentioned it, but she'd thought it'd bring an end to the questions, not have his eyes light up with excitement and curiosity. "Look, I don't want to talk about it."

"Did they catch him?"

"Didn't you understand what I said? Not talking about it. At all." The last thing she needed was the nightmares to return. She pushed the image of plunging the blazing sword into Paili's heart from her mind. An image of herself clinging to Queran's back as she hurled fireballs at his wing tried to creep in to take its place.

"Yeah, but-"

"Did you want something?"

"You weren't at dinner." He barely paused for breath before he continued. "Why did you have an assassin after you?"

"I wasn't hungry." She ignored his second question.

"And the assassin?"

"What time is breakfast?"

"Six to six-thirty. After that you miss out. Now about-"

"Goodnight, Dominic." She strode forward, grasping the edge of the door.

He placed his hand on the front of the door so she couldn't close it. "What happened? With the assassin. Why won't you talk about it? Did you get hurt?"

"No. I'm going to sleep now. Move your hand."

"Was it something to do with becoming a mage?"

She started to close the door. Her eyes narrowed when he resisted. "Move your hand. Now."

"Why won't you answer me?"

She'd had enough. Why did they all have to question her? Feeling the panther prowling inside her, wanting to escape, she let only it's power trickle through, slamming it back as she slammed the door shut. She leaned against the door. It had been close. For a second she'd thought the panther would completely escape.

Dominic hit the door. "That's not the way to make friends. They said to make you feel welcome. Well screw you. Find your own way around."

She listened to his footsteps retreat. Closing her eyes she tried not to think about what she'd just done. He'd been questioning her. What had he expected? She sighed, pushing away from the door. Maybe she'd apologise to him tomorrow. But she wasn't about to spill her guts just to have a friendly face in this place.

Too bad if they all hated her, she wasn't about to stick around any longer than she had to. Turning off the light switch as she passed it, she crossed the room to drop onto her bed. Her stomach rumbled and she felt the panther stir. Breakfast was going to be a long time away.

Pulling out her phone, she sent a text to Kade. *I hate it here.*

What do you want me to do?

Nothing. I'm going to sleep. But I still hate it here.

I'll be there 8 a.m. Monday.

I can't wait.

She set the alarm on her phone and put it on the floor beside her bed. Lying there, she stared at the ceiling, light splashing across it from the still open blind. It took her ages to fall asleep and she woke several times during the night, the strange sounds and scents of the area disturbing her. Twice she had to fight against the panther breaking free. Missing dinner hadn't been a good idea.

It wasn't even six when she gave up on sleep, her room filled with light from her open window. She turned off her alarm, which hadn't had a chance to ring yet, and lay staring at the ceiling wishing she was anywhere but here. It was a waste of time. She didn't want to learn how to kill dragons. She was already far too efficient at that. Reluctantly rising from bed, she grabbed her bag from the wardrobe and wondered where the bathroom was. Maybe she shouldn't have upset Dominic last night. At least not until she'd learned where a few more things were.

Opening her bedroom door, she peered up the hallway. It was empty and quiet. Where was everyone? Going to the next door along, she knocked on it. No one answered. Her hand hovered over the doorknob and she wondered if she should open it. She knocked one more time and waited a few minutes before she opened the door. The room was identical to hers except the bed was made and the room looked like no one was using it. She was almost relieved to see there were bars at the window. Maybe her grandparents hadn't deliberately had some installed just for her. But she bet they would have if there hadn't been any on the window. Closing the door, she looked in each direction. The next door or the one on the other side of her door?

She finally decided to knock on the door on the other side of hers. About to give up, Amber was surprised when the door swung open and Dominic stood in front of her. "Uhm, sorry about last night. I was tired."

He nodded, but remained silent.

"Can you tell me where the bathroom is?"

He pointed up the corridor in the opposite direction to her room. "Fifth door on the right."

"Okay." She started to move away. "Thanks." She heard the door close when she'd taken only a couple of steps. Obviously he wasn't about to forgive her. Either that or he wasn't a morning person, but she didn't think that was the case. As a Knight, not being alert the moment you woke would probably be seen as a weakness.

Once she'd finished in the bathroom, she returned her bag to her wardrobe and knocked on Dominic's door again. He opened it much quicker this time, standing there silently. Amber bit back the urge to tell him to get over himself. That she didn't have to tell him her life story. "Can you show me to the dining room?"

"When I'm ready to go there." He closed the door.

She stared at the white door, fuming. Fine! Let him be like that. It wasn't like she needed to make friends here. She wasn't sticking around any longer than she had to. Striding back to her room, she left her door open, dropping onto the bed. Pulling out her phone she was relieved to see no new messages from Cooper. Maybe she'd finally got through to him that he didn't need to text her every few minutes.

I survived the night. She sent the text to Kade.

Why are you up so early?

Breakfast is only served between 6 and 6:30. Missed dinner. Starving.

Why did you miss dinner? How is the panther handling that?

It felt like the panther was prowling back and forth, barely caged, but telling Kade that probably wasn't a good idea. *Because they've got too many stupid rules here.* She looked up when Dominic appeared in the doorway. *Have to go. My tour guide has arrived to take me to the dining room.*

Be careful.

She smiled. Like he was all the time? Yeah right. She rose to her feet, tucking her phone away, trying to think of something to say to Dominic. He remained silent as they walked along the corridors. She thought of and discarded several comments. If he expected her to tell him about the assassins before he'd talk to her again he was going to be very disappointed.

Chapter Five

It was quiet in the dining hall and Amber glanced around at the kids sitting at the tables, eating. Her eyes momentarily landed on Jennifer who sent her a venomous glare. Great. Just what she needed.

Dominic pushed past her, headed for the far side of the room where a man was serving breakfast. The man was dressed in a black t-shirt and jeans, had his dark brown hair cut very close to his head and his brown eyes took in everything. He stood behind a counter that separated the dining room from the kitchen.

Amber followed Dominic, collecting a tray like he did. She waited behind Dominic while the man added bacon, eggs and toast to a plate and handed it to Dominic along with a glass of water. Moving along, Dominic gathered cutlery off the counter while the man handed Amber a plate of food and a glass of orange juice. Smelling the dragon bone in the juice, she held it out to the man.

He didn't reach for the glass. "Drink your juice."

Dominic, who'd started to move away, turned back.

"No thanks." Amber continued to hold out the glass.

"That wasn't a suggestion. It was an order."

She placed the juice on the counter. "I'm not having dragon bone."

"You can't be a true Knight if you don't."

Amber started to turn away, not interested in continuing an obviously unproductive argument.

"I didn't give you permission to walk away. Drink the juice now. I don't want a single drop left in that glass."

She faced the man. "I won't drink or eat anything with dragon bone in it." She spoke each word slowly, aware of the silence in the dining room behind her. Reaching out with her empty hand, she pushed the glass over. The noise of the glass striking the counter rang out in the silent room. The juice quickly spread.

The man stretched across the counter, knocking the plate from her hands. The plate and food tumbled to the floor. "No juice, no breakfast."

Hunger and anger had the panther wanting to

break free and strike out at the man. "You're really going to want to feed me. I won't be held responsible for what happens if I'm not fed."

The man chuckled. "Nice try, little girl. My orders came from the High Protector himself. Now I'll get you a glass of juice and you'll drink it before I dish up another plate for you."

"I don't think so." She tried to search the building with her mind, but whatever the building was made of, it wouldn't allow her to reach beyond the room she was in. Striding towards the door, she stopped when four kids moved in front of her. She only recognised Jennifer. "Get out of the way."

Jennifer smiled. "No dragons can get in here and rescue you. You're on your own this time."

"I don't need dragons to rescue me. Now get out of my way."

"Or what?" Jennifer's smile became smug. "You're a little outnumbered."

Amber brought fireballs to her hands. "Then how about I deal with that by starting with you?" She heard the gasps of the kids behind her. She had felt them advancing, but now they stopped.

"Jennifer, fetch the High Protector."

"But Stanley–"

"Now."

Jennifer sent Amber a look that warned her there'd be payback, then left the room, shutting the door hard behind her.

Amber stepped to the side so she could keep an eye on everyone. Extinguishing the fireball from one hand, she pulled out her phone and rang Ronan.

"What did you do?"

"It wasn't me. They're trying to make me have dragon bone. I'm not eating it, drinking it, or consuming it in any way, shape or form." To her, dragons were people. And you didn't eat people. It was bad enough that she had to wear the skin of them.

"Hang that phone up now." Stanley pointed a finger at her, coming closer. "No phone calls during class time."

"They're trying to weaken you," Ronan said.

"What?"

"I'm not going to repeat myself," Stanley warned.

Amber kept an eye on him and the kids who fanned out around him. "You better hurry up and explain yourself before all hell breaks loose, Ronan."

"Dragons can't eat dragon bone. That includes mages. Blood, flesh, organs, but no bone. It weakens us. They would know that. Tell them if they force something harmful on you it's an act of war. We'll bring two castles full of warriors against them. Their Brisbane headquarters would be rubble within hours."

"That's it." Stanley started to step forward, his hand reaching for the phone.

Amber disconnected, slid her phone into her pocket and sidestepped him. "You better wait for the High Protector before you begin a war he might not want to start." Her phone rang and she ignored it. "Back away."

The door burst open and Jennifer entered the room, followed by Martin and Charles. Amber's phone continued to ring.

"Turn that phone off," Martin ordered.

"Actually you might want me to answer it." Amber kept the fireball in her hand. "Otherwise you'll have two castles worth of dragons attacking very soon." The phone stopped ringing and immediately started again.

"What have you done?" Charles demanded.

"Protected myself."

"Get these children out of here," Martin ordered Stanley before he turned to Amber. "Answer that phone."

Amber smiled as Jennifer was sent from the room, protesting. As soon as it was only her and the three men, she extinguished the fireball and answered the phone. "Yeah?"

"What's going on?"

"I haven't figured that out yet."

Martin held out his hand. "Give me the phone."

"I'll take it." Charles also held out a hand.

"You're no longer the High Protector. This is my concern. You brought her here and put everyone at risk."

"Who do you want to speak to, Ronan? My grandfather or Martin, the High Protector? There's some arguing going on over who's running the show."

"In that case put Charles on the phone."

She almost laughed, but the situation was still too dangerous for that. She held out the phone to her grandfather. "He wants to talk to you."

"This is outrageous," Martin said.

Stanley stood by quietly, watching everything carefully. Amber didn't blame him. She was warily watching everyone too. Especially Stanley. Her stomach growled and she bit back the growl the panther wanted her to make. They better sort this out quickly or she'd be finding her own meal.

After saying yes a couple of times and no once, Charles handed the phone back to Amber. "Yes?"

"You will ring me in an hour and tell me if everything has been sorted to your satisfaction."

"Okay."

"And whatever you do, don't have any of the dragon bone."

"You could have told me about that earlier."

"You had already refused it. I didn't expect them to force the issue. Especially since harming you means they lose your time."

"So if I had eaten it I–"

"Would have been a willing participant. It's only if they'd managed to force you. Now go and finish sorting them out, kitten. I'll hear from you in an hour."

When Ronan hung up, she returned her phone to her pocket. "I need breakfast."

"You will eat once we sort this out," Martin said.

"If I'm not fed soon, I'll be hunting down my own breakfast and I don't think the wild animal I turn into will care what gets in the way."

"Stanley, serve her breakfast," Charles ordered.

"Stanley, don't move until this is sorted." Martin kept his gaze on Amber. "A bird isn't going to hunt down anything that can be found within this building."

Amber grinned, trying to imitate Ronan's predatory one. "I wasn't planning to turn into a bird."

"Panther," Charles said.

Martin rounded on him. "What?"

"She turns into a damned panther."

"Why didn't you tell me?"

"Because I couldn't volunteer any information about her or the dragons, but since she's about to disclose it herself it doesn't matter." Charles' gaze went to Stanley. "Get her food. Immediately!"

Stanley nodded, returning to his counter. Amber followed him, taking the plate he held out, breathing in the scent of the food. It was safe. No dragon bone at all. She sat at one of the tables, quickly finishing what was on her plate and returning for seconds. Skipping dinner hadn't been a good idea. But it had meant she'd learned some valuable information. Her grandfather wouldn't break his word and Martin wasn't to be trusted no matter what he said.

Leaving the dirty plate on the table, Amber rejoined the three men who were arguing in hushed tones near the door. She was tempted to tell them they'd have to talk quieter than that if they didn't want her to hear.

"Ring your dragon," Charles ordered. "Tell him you're safe."

"Am I?"

Charles nodded abruptly.

She turned her gaze to Martin. "Well?"

"For now."

She held Martin's gaze a moment longer before she took out her phone and rang Ronan.

"All sorted?"

"I'm safe. For now."

"I want regular calls. If anything else happens you'll have bodyguards."

"They won't let dragons in here, Ronan."

"Human ones. Ex military."

"Isn't that a bit overkill?"

"I love some of the words you humans come up with. Overkill. You can never kill too much. Ring me at midday."

Ronan hung up before Amber could tell him that wasn't what she'd meant. She didn't want anyone killed. Holding back a sigh, she returned her phone to her pocket, her gaze travelling to each man who still stared at her. "What now?"

"Classes," Charles said.

"Who's going to want a mage in their class?" Martin asked. "It's a bad idea. She's already made up her mind which side she's on."

"I'm on my side. That'll never change," Amber said.

"I'll take her." Stanley smiled.

Amber was glad she'd had plenty of practice at not retreating from Ronan's smiles. Stanley's smile promised revenge. She met his gaze without flinching. "What do you think you can teach me?"

"How to treat your superiors with respect. Eventually. But we'll start with hand to hand combat."

"Hand to hand combat sounds okay." Especially with the amount of people who tended to put her on their list of people they wanted dead. And unlike the handful of kids who'd told her to drop dead over the years, these people had the means to make her death a possibility.

"Follow me." Stanley swung open the door.

"Amber."

About to step through the door, she looked over her shoulder at her grandfather, waiting for him to continue speaking.

Charles held her gaze a moment before he spoke. "I'll see you after you've eaten lunch. Have Dominic bring you to my quarters."

She nodded then followed Stanley who led her through corridors to yet another closed door. What was it they had about keeping all their doors shut? There was probably no point in asking though. Not with the mood Stanley was in.

When they entered the room, six kids came to attention. She only knew Jennifer and Dominic. The middle of the room was covered in thick exercise mats. Hand to hand combat suddenly didn't look so good.

Stanley moved to the front of the room, standing with his legs planted firmly apart, his arms crossed over his chest. "Josephine." His gaze fell on a girl that reminded Amber of Dominic with her white blond hair, short like nearly everyone else in the room, and her blue eyes.

The girl stepped forward. "Yes?"

"I'll partner you. Everyone else pair off. Hand to hand. No weapons."

"But Stanley," a boy, with a shaved head and hazel eyes, protested. "We're meant to be doing sword work today."

"Who is in charge of this class, Wheeler?"

"You are. But why aren't we doing sword work?"

"Because we have a new student who can't use a sword."

"Then why isn't she in the little kids' class?" Josephine asked.

Stanley smiled. The same one he'd used earlier that had made Amber think revenge was coming. "Because I think we can teach her a lot more in this class."

Amber looked at all the kids nodding, smiling in agreement. And her grandfather had told her to give them a chance. It looked like they weren't about to give her one.

Jennifer half raised a hand. "I'll partner Amber." She sent her used car salesman smile in Amber's direction.

Amber nearly groaned. Oh great. Maybe her grandfather should have given Jennifer the lecture on giving people chances because it looked like she'd got Stanley's message loud and clear.

Chapter Six

Jennifer waited until everyone else paired up before she attacked Amber. Within seconds, Amber was on the mat, trying not to wince from Jennifer's rough treatment. She healed herself as she rose to her feet, wishing she could use fireballs. Then it'd be Jennifer losing, not her.

"You're not even trying," Stanley called out to Amber.

"It might help if you actually tried to teach me something."

"You're a mage, shouldn't you have some skills in fighting? Or don't dragons believe in letting mages learn how to fight?"

Stanley's words caused her hands to curl into fists. Glaring at him, she opened one and held it out, letting a fireball form. "They let us fight with more dangerous weapons than fists."

"Used properly, fists can be just as dangerous as your little balls of fire."

She fought the urge to demand he prove it. The dragons' competitiveness must be wearing off on her. "You have to get close and risk being harmed to kill with bare hands. I can stay out of your reach and kill you from a distance."

"Only if you're accurate." Stanley pointed to a tall, wiry boy with light brown hair, green eyes and a sprinkling of freckles. "Oliver, bring the practice dummy." He then turned to the boy who'd been Oliver's partner. A dark skinned, broad shouldered boy with a shaved head and dark brown eyes. "And you can bring a fire extinguisher, Roy."

Both boys left the room and Amber began to wonder if it was wise to show them what she could do. A stationary target was simple after fighting moving ones. But did she really want them to know what she was capable of? Ronan would tell her not to show any weakness, but he was a dragon and she was currently dealing with humans.

Roy returned first, holding out the extinguisher to Stanley who shook his head. "Put out any fires she starts."

Oliver entered next, lugging the practice dummy that was mostly made of wood. He set it up at the front of the classroom, near Stanley, before he rejoined his classmates on the mat.

Stanley stepped well away from the dummy before he gestured towards it. "Go ahead. Take him out." He smiled.

The mocking tone and disbelieving smile had Amber throw a fireball first at the dummy's legs and then at its head. She smiled as Stanley's smile disappeared. "Was that all?" She almost added a sir, but thought that might be a bit too much.

Roy stepped forward with the extinguisher, putting out the flames that leapt around the dummy. As soon as they were extinguished, he stepped well back.

"Big deal," Jennifer said. "Any of us could do that if we were mages. We could even do that with lit arrows. Do you want me to show you?"

Stanley shook his head, his gaze returning to Amber. "Why did you hit the legs first?"

She hesitated then decided to tell him part of the truth. "To disable him. So he couldn't run either to me or away from me." If it had been a real battle, she would have let him live. She didn't kill if she didn't have to and even then she still tried to avoid it.

Stanley nodded. "Swap partners and go again. Show's over."

This time she was paired with Roy. She eyed his broad shoulders warily. He gestured for her to attack so she did, expecting to land on the mats. She ended up sprawled on her back, but the impact wasn't anywhere near as hard as when Jennifer had slammed her into the mats. She didn't even need to heal herself. Rising to her feet, she met Roy's gaze, wondering why he was going easy on her.

Several more times Roy landed her on the mats, then he started to explain to her what she was doing wrong and show her what she should do instead. The next time she attacked, Amber nearly managed to stay on her feet.

Stanley stepped away from Dominic, who he was practising with, and strode over to stand in front of Roy. "Who is teaching this class?"

"You are."

"Then focus on what you're meant to be doing. Attack."

Roy nodded once before he faced Amber. This time she lasted on her feet a little longer. As she went down, Roy's elbow smashed into her nose, causing a nosebleed. She reached up her hand and healed it, wiping away the blood as she rose to her feet.

"What did you do?" Stanley demanded.

"Tried to stay on my feet," Amber said.

"No." He pointed to her nose. "What did you do?"

"It was Roy's elbow that caused the nosebleed, not me."

"You can heal?"

Amber shrugged. Surely they'd already known. She remembered her grandfather's words to Martin. Okay, maybe they hadn't.

"That's why they want you, isn't it?"

Again she shrugged.

"Dragon Mages can't heal humans. How can you?"

The words 'I'm not human' came to mind and she instantly discarded them. "I can only heal dragons and Dragon Mages."

"What about Knights?"

She thought of the dragon bone they consumed. Maybe it'd work like the dragon blood did for mages. "I don't know."

Stanley drew a knife from his boot. "Roy, give me your arm."

Amber stared at Stanley. Surely he wasn't about to harm Roy just to see if she could heal him.

"Now, Roy. How many of my orders are you going to disobey in one day?"

Roy started to raise his arm and Amber realised what was different about him. She couldn't smell any dragon bone. "No. I can't heal him." She stepped between Roy and Stanley.

"You just finished telling me you don't know. So what's changed in a matter of seconds?"

"I can't smell dragon bone on him."

"Of course you can. It's probably faint because it's been a week," Stanley said.

Roy stepped around her, holding out his arm. "It's okay. I'm willing to be the test subject. Stanley's right. It's been a week since I've had dragon bone so that's probably why you can barely smell it."

She knew he was lying. Could smell he was. Everyone else in the room smelled of dragon bone. Everyone except him. She reached out, pushing his arm down and met Stanley's gaze. "He might be willing, but I'm not. I'm here to learn, not perform tricks like some circus animal. That wasn't part of the deal I made."

Stanley's lips pressed together and he stared at her for a moment before he called Dominic over. "You practice with Roy. I'll teach the Dragon Mage."

Amber didn't like the sound of that. It had sounded far too much like a threat. And after she landed on the mats several times she began to believe it had been one. He was a lot harder on her than Jennifer had been and she'd thought that had been bad.

By the time the class stopped for lunch, Amber had needed to draw power from one of her bracelets that she always wore for storing extra power. She started to cross the room to ask Dominic to show her to her grandfather's quarters then changed her mind, aiming for Roy who was hurrying out the door. Catching up with him in the corridor, she tugged on his arm. "Roy."

He shook her off. "I didn't need your help back there."

She kept her voice quiet. "You don't have any dragon bone in your blood. None."

Roy stopped walking and faced her. "You can't know that."

Grabbing his arm, she lifted it and inhaled deeply. "Yeah, I can know that." She let him draw his arm away, trying to figure out what he did smell like.

"Then why didn't you say something? I won't let you blackmail me."

"I need someone to show me to my grandfather's quarters."

Roy frowned. "Why?"

"He told me to see him after I've eaten. So I need someone to take me to the dining room and then to his quarters when I'm finished. Oh, and probably take me to wherever we're meant to go next."

"You could have got anyone to do that. Why me?"

Her reason almost made her cringe. She was becoming too much like a dragon. "Because you owe me."

"I don't owe you anything."

"Why don't you take dragon bone?"

"What else are you going to expect? Look, I didn't mean to hurt you. That was an accident."

Amber shook her head. "I'm not looking for payback for a nosebleed. You weren't as rough as Jennifer. Or Stanley."

"Then what do you want?"

"All I need is someone to show me where I have to go. Someone who's not going to sulk if I don't answer their questions."

Roy grinned momentarily, almost reluctantly. "That sounds like Dominic."

"Yeah. So, will you?"

"I suppose." He turned back the way they'd come.

"What's this way?" Amber pointed to the corridor ahead of them.

"Dining room." He walked a little faster.

She gestured behind them. "What's that way?"

"My room. Is this the way it's going to be? You can ask questions, but I can't."

"Do you need to go to your room first? I can wait."

Roy shook his head. "I don't need to any more."

"Do you have dragon bone in there?"

He shook his head again. "No."

"Then–" she broke off, coming to a complete stop, staring at him.

Roy stopped, slowly turning to face her. "What?"

She had to be wrong. It was impossible. Crossing the several steps between them, she reached for his arm again. He tried to draw away from her, but she stepped even closer, breathing in the scent of his skin. "Dragon." She spoke the word so quietly there was almost no sound.

Roy clamped a hand over her mouth. "No. Don't you dare accuse me of that."

Amber pulled away from him, seeing fear in his eyes. "Why are you here?"

"My parents have been Knights their entire lives. My grandparents and great-grandparents were Knights."

"Roy–"

"No. You're mistaken. Maybe it's the dragon bone you can smell."

She heard fear in his voice, could smell his fear. There was no way he'd admit to it, even if it was true. It shouldn't be true, but he smelled faintly like dragon. Like the kind of dragon that Shylah was. Part human, part dragon, but the smell wasn't as strong on him. "You're probably right. Dragon bone. Very faint."

Roy froze for a second then drew back from her. "Yes, dragon bone. I'll… I'll show you to the dining room."

Amber nodded, her mind spinning with questions. What was going on? And what was she meant to do about it? Ronan! She'd have to tell him. But not right now. Not where other people could hear her.

When they reached the dining room, it was to find everyone already seated and eating. Amber collected a tray and took the plate Stanley handed her. She inhaled deeply before she added it to her tray, collecting a drink of water and cutlery before she sat at the end of a half empty table. Across the room Roy sat, sending her frequent glances. He knew. He'd have to know. And that would be why he avoided dragon bone. It weakened dragons. She couldn't stop wondering how a dragon, even part dragon, had become a Knight. They hated dragons.

Once her meal was finished, she rose to her feet, noticing Roy do the same, leaving his half eaten meal on the table as he headed for the door. Amber crossed the room, stepping through the doorway just after him. They walked silently through the corridors and she didn't bother finding something to talk about. She was too busy trying to figure out how he'd ended up a Knight. How the impossible had happened.

Roy stopped partway along a hallway, gesturing to the door a couple of metres away from them. "Your grandfather's quarters."

Amber stared at him a moment, trying to see any other indications that he was a dragon. She was unable to find any, but she also couldn't when the dragons she knew were in human form. "Will you wait?"

Roy nodded.

She hurried forward and knocked on the door. She hoped this wouldn't take long because she still needed to ring Ronan.

Charles opened the door, stepping back so she could enter. He closed it firmly behind him. "What did you think you were doing earlier? Why have you got to make such a scene all the time?"

"I can't have dragon bone. You know that."

"I didn't know what they had planned. I didn't agree to it. You're of no use to us if you're weak. All I ask is that you don't make a scene. You could have handled things better."

Her eyes narrowed. "Don't you dare blame this on

me. I wasn't the one trying to force someone to have something that was no good for them."

Charles pointed a finger at her. "Don't bring shame on our family."

Amber crossed her arms over her chest. It wasn't fair. He was acting like it was all her fault. She shouldn't have been surprised. "Was that it? Can I go?"

Charles stared at her for nearly a minute before he nodded his head.

Chapter Seven

Amber spun, flung the door open and let it slam shut behind her. Roy was still in the hallway. "Take me to my room." Roy silently led the way and Amber was relieved. She was too angry to talk and needed the time to calm down before she rang Ronan. At her doorway, she again asked, "Will you wait?" When Roy nodded, she entered her room and closed her door. Sitting on the edge of her still unmade bed, she rang Ronan.

"It's after midday."

"I had to eat. You didn't want me to turn into a panther and attack them, did you?"

Her question was greeted by silence.

"Well?"

"I'm thinking."

Amber shook her head, a slight smile forming. "It's

not going to happen, Ronan. You can quit fantasising about it."

"Have you learned anything useful in their Knight school?"

She eyed the door, wondering how good Roy's hearing was. "Depends on what you term useful."

"You have? Tell me."

"Hang on." Amber crossed the room, still keeping the phone fairly close to her mouth, and opened the door. "Roy, what's planned for this afternoon?"

"Archery lessons."

"Great. Where are they held? We aren't late, are we?"

Roy shook his head. "The minibus doesn't leave for about another twenty minutes."

"Minibus? We're leaving the headquarters?"

Roy nodded.

"Thanks." She closed the door again, leaning against the wall. "Ronan?"

"Chait will follow you."

"Okay."

"Ring me when you can talk without someone listening in."

"If that's ever possible." She returned her phone to her pocket, momentarily closing her eyes. How was she going to manage six weeks of this? It was far worse than she'd expected it to be. Pushing away from the wall, she opened the door again. "Okay, I'm ready."

The walk to the front of the building was made in silence and they stepped outside to find the rest of their class standing around waiting. Stanley drove up several minutes later in a black minibus and they all piled inside. Amber sat in the back row next to Roy, who didn't look happy with that arrangement. Well, she wasn't happy either. Why couldn't she just go home? Why did everyone have to demand so much of her all the time? She stared out the window, hoping that Chait was able to keep track of her.

By the time they'd finished at the archery range, Amber was ready to murder someone. Probably her grandfather for putting her in this situation. She leaned her head against the minibus window, once again sitting in the back row with a disgruntled Roy. Archery wasn't her thing and Stanley had delighted in pointing that out. So had Josephine, who she'd learned was the oldest of the group at twenty and was Dominic's sister. Yet another relative she didn't need. Jennifer and Oliver were both eighteen while Dominic, Roy and Wheeler were her age, seventeen.

While they'd been at the archery range, Alsandair had momentarily appeared out of the Void, gathered her arrows from the target and then a minute later reappeared near her. He'd given her the arrows with a wink. "Chait's here too." Then he'd disappeared back into the Void, leaving angry Knights complaining about her bringing dragons onto their turf. She didn't know whether to feel better that Ronan had two Golds watching her or worried that he thought she needed two.

They arrived back in time for dinner and afterwards, Amber asked Roy to show her to her room. When they reached her door, she asked, "Where's your room?"

He pointed down the corridor. "Last door on the right."

"Okay." She stepped into her room, closing the door to lean against the wall. She'd begun to think the day would never end and she still had another one to get through. Not to mention another five weeks after this one. She was never going to survive it.

Crossing the room, she looked out the barred window, checking the space between the bars with her hands. It didn't even look like she'd be able to fit through them by turning into a goshawk. She was stuck in this building until Monday morning. It felt like an eternity.

Dropping onto her still unmade bed, she called Ronan.

"Can you talk?"

"I don't know."

"Is there anyone with you?"

"No, but that doesn't mean no one's listening."

"Is it important? Do I need to know about it urgently?"

Amber thought for a minute. "No, I don't think so." At least she hoped not.

"I'll talk to you Monday morning."

"Kade is collecting me."

"Not anymore."

Amber glared at the phone when Ronan disconnected. She was tempted to ring him back, but knew it would be a waste of time. Ronan wasn't about to listen. He'd already made up his mind. Rising, she grabbed her bag and headed for the bathroom to shower before bed.

When she finally made it to bed, she lay awake, staring at the ceiling in the darkened room. She sent a text message to Kade letting him know that Ronan had changed their plans and that she was going to bed. Once he'd replied, telling her goodnight, she dropped her phone on the floor and rolled to her side, tucking her arm under her head. The bed was too small and the room too quiet. She missed Kade, even though he took up most of the space in bed. Closing her eyes, she tried to sleep. It took ages before she fell asleep, frequently waking through the night to unfamiliar sounds.

The next morning, Amber reluctantly dragged herself from bed, not wanting to face the day. Once she'd sent a text to both Kade and Ronan she used the bathroom before heading to Roy's room. She was glad she didn't have to hassle Dominic to show her where the dining room was. Roy answered on the first knock.

"Morning."

He nodded in greeting, stepping out of his room and closing the door behind him.

"Why are all the doors shut?" He took so long to answer Amber began to think he wasn't going to.

"Tidiness."

"Tidiness?"

Roy nodded.

Amber shook her head. "That makes no sense."

Roy shrugged.

"Tidiness." She sent a look to Roy who continued to walk beside her, his gaze straight ahead. This time he didn't reply, not even with a shrug or a nod of his head. She was still trying to figure it out when they reached the dining room a minute later. She didn't believe him, certain there was another reason.

Roy increased his pace, headed for Stanley who was serving the kids lined up in front of him. Amber didn't bother to pick up her pace. Roy could have his space, for now.

Once again, Roy sent her frequent glances, heading for the door the moment he saw she was finished. Amber rose from the table, striding across the room, ignoring the looks from the kids she walked past. It didn't look like any of them were happy to have her here, not even the younger ones. Stepping into the corridor, she saw Roy had waited for her. He walked off the moment she saw him. Even though she hurried to catch up, Roy continued to stay slightly ahead of her. She didn't know whether to laugh or shake her head, but at least he didn't try and lose her. They reached the classroom before anyone else and Roy drew his sword that hung at his side, practising manoeuvres.

Amber watched him, trying to memorise his movements. It was impossible. He was too fast. She didn't know if she should be watching his feet or his hands. She was nowhere near ready for this class. And Stanley had known that. Even her grandfather had to have known. He'd seen her fight. They wanted her to fail. She straightened her shoulders. "Show me."

Roy looked in her direction, his gaze dropping to her side where no sword hung.

"You can show me the actions. I don't need a sword." She was probably better off without one for now. At least until she knew what to do with it. An image of her sword bursting into flames came to mind and she pushed that thought away. That wasn't the way a sword was meant to be used.

Roy slowed down his movements, waiting for a while after each action. Amber stood beside him, watching and matching her own movements to his. They had been at it for several minutes when the door swung open and the rest of the students entered, Stanley following them.

"Think you're ready for a sword now, do you?" Stanley stood in the doorway, hands on his hips.

Amber stopped when Roy sped up his movements. "What do you think?" Her words dripped with sarcasm.

"Roy, fetch one of the practice swords since you think she's up to it."

Amber nearly swore, instead she kept her expression neutral, not daring to look in Roy's direction. She continued to hold Stanley's gaze as he stepped out of the doorway so Roy could exit the room. "That's surprising."

"What is?" Stanley demanded.

"Your faith in my abilities." She smiled when Stanley glared at her.

Stanley strode further into the room. "All of you. Pair off. Swords out."

Roy came back into the room, carrying a second sword. He held it out to Stanley.

"Give it to the mage. You pair with her since you're so keen to help her." Stanley gestured towards Amber before he pointed a finger at Oliver. "Over here. You can practice with me."

Amber took the sword Roy handed her, his eyes narrowed as he glared at her. Raising her sword, she gestured for him to begin.

He glared at her a moment longer before he started to attack. Within minutes he had her unarmed and his sword pressed against her neck. He held it there a bit longer before he stepped back and nodded towards her sword on the floor.

Keeping a wary eye on him, Amber picked up her sword, mimicking Roy's stance. He attacked and she blocked. Again it was only minutes before he had his sword at her throat. Anger rushed through her. What was her grandfather thinking letting her be put in this class?

"Enough." Stanley strode towards them. "Roy, you pair up with Oliver. Jennifer, you train with the mage."

Amber struggled to keep her expression neutral, especially when Stanley grinned. There was no way Jennifer would go easy on her. Her grin matched Stanley's in its level of satisfaction and Amber quickly raised her sword.

Jennifer came at her with rapid attacks and Amber was forced to retreat. Slipping to one side, she barely escaped being cut by the sword. Anger rushed through her as she jumped back from another wild attack. The panther stirred, wanting to escape. Then her anger exploded and the sword burst into flames. Jennifer stumbled and Amber cut her arm, the skin instantly searing. The smell of burnt flesh filled the room as she tried to regain her balance.

"Stop," Stanley bellowed.

Amber wanted to demand why he stopped the fight for Jennifer, but not for her. Instead, she didn't speak, lowering her sword and forcing the flames away.

"Fix her." Stanley's gaze was on Amber, his finger pointing to Jennifer. "Go on."

Roy took the sword from Amber as she took half a step forward. She looked towards him, trying to read his expression, but he turned away from her. She closed the distance between her and Jennifer, reaching out her hands to place them over the burnt flesh.

"What if I don't want her to heal me?" Jennifer demanded.

"We need to know if she can," Stanley said. "Now stay still."

Amber closed her eyes as she tried to focus on finding the dragon bone in Jennifer's body to use it to heal her. It didn't work. She tried several different techniques and nothing helped. Letting go of Jennifer, she took a step back. "I can't heal her."

"Try harder," Stanley said.

"I did try. Dragon bone isn't enough to heal with."

"Give it another go."

Amber met Stanley's glare with one of her own. "I've. Tried. Everything. There's nothing I can do to heal her."

"Then what's the good of you?"

There was probably only one thing they could relate to. "I can kill dragons."

Roy started to step back from Amber only to halt his action.

"Jennifer, go to the first aid room. Everyone else, back to practice. Josephine, you pair up with the mage.

Chapter Eight

By the time they stopped for lunch, Amber was so angry she didn't think she could even speak to Ronan. Instead, she sent him a text telling him she was alive. Her phone rang and she stared at it, seated at the table that had emptied the moment she'd sat at it. She really couldn't talk to Ronan, not without abusing him and telling him he should have made a better deal for her. As soon as her phone stopped ringing, she sent another text. *Busy*. Her phone remained silent and she finished eating her meal, rising from the table to follow Roy when he left the room.

The afternoon wasn't much better than the morning. By the time Roy walked her down the corridor to her room, after dinner, she was ready to tell Ronan he might as well kill all the Knights. They were worse than dragons. She'd actually prefer to spend a week with Flinn than to spend an afternoon with Stanley and Jennifer. Or even a month with him. Stopping in front of her door, she removed the post–it note stuck to it.

"Where's the training room?" She held the note out to Roy.

He swung her door open and looked into her room.

"What are you doing?" Amber tugged the door shut again, blocking out the sight of her unmade bed.

"You should have kept your room tidy." He turned away and started walking down the corridor.

Amber hurried after him, pushing the note into her pocket. "It is tidy." Didn't she always put her bag back in the wardrobe?

"Your bed isn't made."

"So? Who's going to see it?"

Roy ignored her, turning into another corridor. After leading her along several corridors he eventually opened a door and gestured inside. "I'll be back in an hour."

"Wait." She reached out for him, but he dodged her hand. "What if I'm not that long?"

Roy smiled. "You will be." His smile faded and he strode away.

Amber watched his retreating back, wishing he hadn't left her here alone. What did it matter? She didn't need him. Whatever it was that was about to happen she'd manage. Entering the room, she looked around, surprised to see Martin and Josephine standing in the middle of an extremely large room. Around the outside a four-lane track was painted on the floor, while various types of gym equipment were set up in the middle. She walked across the room, stopping in front of them. Her hands remained by her side, ready to call up fireballs if necessary.

"Jog around the track for an hour. In future keep your room tidy." Martin started to leave.

"What?"

"Don't act dumb. You heard me." Martin kept walking.

She hadn't been acting dumb. She just couldn't believe such a stupid punishment. "My room wasn't messy."

Martin left the room, not even glancing in her direction.

Josephine pointed to the track. "I don't have all night. You better get started or you can do two hours and I'll get someone else to watch you."

"There's no way I'm spending an hour jogging around in circles for no good reason." She crossed her arms over her chest, her eyes narrowing. "And you can't make me."

Josephine smiled. "What makes you think you're so special that you don't have to abide by our rules? I don't care whose granddaughter you are. If one of the teachers said your room was messy, then it was messy. Now get started."

Her jaw tightened as she kept back the words she wanted to shout. The only teacher likely to make a complaint was Stanley. Spinning on her heel she strode to the edge of the room. It wasn't fair. What was the big deal about making the bed? You only unmade it again at night. She started to jog slowly, barely little more than a walk.

By the time the hour was over, Amber was fuming. Finding Roy in the corridor didn't cheer her up, especially since he looked to be in the best mood she'd seen him in since she'd learned his secret. Just great. Everyone was having a marvellous time and all she wanted to do was go home. Tomorrow. She couldn't wait. The moment it was eight, she was out of here.

After Roy left her at her room, she grabbed her bag, used the bathroom and sent a text to Kade and Ronan. She still wasn't in the mood to talk to anyone. The only thing she was likely to do was get in a fight with them. And that probably wasn't a good idea when it came to Ronan. Exhausted, she fell almost instantly asleep. But still she woke on and off throughout the night. She doubted she'd ever get used to this place.

After breakfast the next day, Roy took Amber to the training room where all the kids were using the gym equipment. She stood in the doorway, wishing she didn't have to be here. At least she'd only be stuck doing this once a week and not five times a week like the rest of them. They could keep their stupid Knight school. There were far too many rules for her.

Stanley, who'd been standing talking to three other men, strode towards her. "What are you waiting for? An invitation? If you don't know how to use the equipment you can jog around the track." He smiled. "I hear you know how to do that. Of a fashion."

She pressed her lips together, refusing to answer. Heading for the closest piece of equipment that wasn't in use, Amber hopped on an exercise bike, slowly pedalling. Eight a.m. better hurry up and arrive. This was ridiculous. The dragons hadn't expected all this from her. Why should the Knights? It wasn't like she planned to make a career fighting dragons. And if she did have to fight them, it wouldn't be like this. She'd use fireballs. Pulling out her phone, she set her alarm for ten to eight. She wasn't sticking around any longer than she had to.

When her alarm sounded, Amber hurried to Roy's

side where he was lifting weights. "I need you to show me to my room and then the front door."

Without speaking, he led her to her room and waited in the corridor. Amber dressed for school, grabbed her bag and, after checking that her bed still looked tidy, stepped into the corridor.

"Can you meet me in the reception room tomorrow afternoon to show me where the class is? I'll be there at four."

"You should learn your way around yourself. It's not that hard." He walked off.

Amber hurried after him, wondering if she should ask him again. How was she meant to find anything around here? She needed a map. A proper one, not the stupid drawing Dominic had given her.

Roy opened the door to the reception room. When she would have thanked him, he spun on his heel and left. She stared at the closed door for a moment before she walked to the front door. Opening it she stared outside, wondering if Ronan was there yet. Hoping he was, she left the building, letting the door close behind her.

She scanned the area. Everything was still. Moving away from the building, she continued to look for Ronan. When she was several metres away from the headquarters he appeared out of the Void in the shadow of the fig tree she'd arrived under Friday afternoon.

He remained standing there, holding out a hand. "Hurry up. Unless you like it here so much you don't want to leave."

Amber quickly crossed the space between them, taking his hand. "Not likely."

Ronan took them through the Void, bringing them out at his water garden. "What happened?"

She eyed Ronan. If he had the information, what would he do with it? Probably nothing good. "This is my information. I own it. I'm only sharing it with you because you're my ally." And also because she didn't know what to do with it, but she wasn't about to tell him that.

"Then hurry up and tell me or I'll start to think you're angling for some sort of exchange."

"You will keep this information to yourself unless there's danger to me from the Knights. And even then you aren't to use it unless it'll benefit us."

"Knowledge is power. I'm not about to throw power away for no good reason."

"One of the Knights is part dragon." She watched Ronan carefully, seeing his expression go blank. She smiled. "Interesting, huh?"

"Has the Knight been put there as a spy?"

She shrugged. "I don't know. I haven't been able to get any information out of him yet."

"There has to be a way to use this."

"Not without my permission or unless you're using it to save my life."

"I already agreed, didn't I?"

"Not really."

"And yet you still gave me the information."

She pointed a finger at him. "Don't cross me, Ronan."

He stepped close, his lips twisting into a predatory smile. "How can I? We're allies. Permanent allies."

"Don't you forget it." She dropped her arm, not wanting to get into an argument with Ronan after the weekend she'd had. "Take me home. I've got school today."

Ronan nodded and grabbed her by the arm. Taking her through the Void, he left her on Kade's verandah, vanishing back into the Void.

Cooper, who'd been sitting on the edge of a railing rushed forward. "You're safe? They didn't hurt you?"

Amber sidestepped, holding up a hand to halt him, dropping her bag on the floor. "I'm fine. I hated it there, but I'll survive."

Kade came out the front door, leaving it open behind him as he crossed the verandah to wrap his arms around her. "I don't like not being around to guard you when you're surrounded by enemies. At least Chait was there to watch you."

Amber pulled back slightly so she could meet his gaze. This was the moment she'd dreaded. Why did it have to occur so soon after getting home? "Ahh, about that."

Kade drew away from her. "What about it?"

Maira stepped outside, Brann close behind her. "You're back." Her welcoming grin faded as she looked from one to the other. "What happened?"

"Well, Amber?" Kade asked.

"The headquarters isn't a normal building. Well, it's a normal building, but I guess it's not made normally."

"Amber." There was a warning in Kade's voice.

"Dragon's can't stay in the Void inside it."

"You're only just telling me this now?"

"I'll go finish getting ready for school." Maira hurried away, Brann and Cooper on her heels.

"Well?"

Amber crossed her arms. "Ronan knew."

"So!"

"What could you have done? Nothing. I was safe." She'd tell him about the dragon bone incident later.

"You don't know that. They could be planning anything. You're not going back."

Amber grinned at him, stepping forward to wrap her arms around his waist. "I missed you too."

"I'm serious."

"I made a deal. There's only five more weekends to get through."

"And weekdays."

"They're only a couple of hours each. Easy compared to an entire weekend." At least she hoped. She rested her head against him. "Can we forget about them for a bit? I don't want to think about the Knights again until tomorrow afternoon." It was impossible to keep the weariness from her voice.

Kade's arms went around her, holding her tight. "Was it that bad? What happened?"

She guessed later had arrived. "I couldn't find the dining room Friday night and missed dinner. Saturday morning they tried to make me eat dragon bone and Sunday I cut Jennifer during sword practice."

"She probably deserved it. And you better not have eaten any dragon bone."

"No, Ronan's already told me it weakens dragons and mages."

"I'll go with you in future."

Amber pulled away from him, shaking her head. "Are you crazy? They'd kill you."

"I don't want you there on your own."

"Too bad."

They were still glaring at each other when Maira came outside, holding Amber's schoolbag out to her. "Time for school or we'll be late."

"We'll finish this later," Kade warned.

Amber picked up her bag and tossed it to Cooper who had followed Maira onto the verandah. "Put that in my room." She took the schoolbag from Maira and followed her to the car, Kade beside her. "I need a sword."

"You've already got one." Kade slid into the car after her.

"It's too heavy for me. I need one I can use." And one that didn't remind her of killing Paili every time she looked at it.

"You could ask Rian to see what we've got at Temolae Keep. There's probably all sorts of weapons in the armoury."

Amber pulled out her phone. "Good idea." She typed in a message and sent it to Rian. *I need a sword. One light enough I can use.* She rested her head against Kade, not looking forward to a day of school. Not long now and she'd be finished. Maybe she should take a year off before she thought about uni. Life was too crazy these days to even think about adding anything else to the already long list of things that needed to be done. A list that seemed to grow longer instead of shorter.

Chapter Nine

Amber's arms tightened around Kade, not wanting to let him go. Tuesday, Wednesday and Thursday afternoon hadn't been too bad. She'd known she wouldn't be at the headquarters long and Kade was waiting for her. They'd argued over it, but he hadn't listened. So the previous afternoons she'd had three dragons waiting in the Void. But today was different. Today she'd once again be stuck at the headquarters for an entire weekend. She wouldn't see Kade again until eight a.m. Monday. That was ages away.

"We can't stand out here all afternoon. Someone's sure to call the cops since you decided to wear your sword." Kade continued to hold onto her.

"I'm not about to walk in there unarmed."

"You're never unarmed."

"Yeah well, I feel better having a sword as well as fireballs."

Ronan stepped out of the Void. "I have better things to do with my afternoon than watch you two. Get inside, kitten."

Amber let her arm, that she'd raised, fall to her side. At least she hadn't called up a fireball. A glance around showed no humans, but when she mentally searched the nearby buildings she found some. "You don't need to be here."

"Inside so I can go." Ronan's gaze was drawn to the sword hanging at Amber's side. "Where did you get that?" He gestured towards it.

"Rian."

"I thought I recognised it. I'm surprised he parted with it."

"He hasn't. He said I could use it until he could have another one made for me." It was still a little heavy for her, but not as bad as the one she'd used to kill Paili.

"It's a good blade. Now get inside."

She resisted the urge to argue with Ronan and looked up at Kade. "I'll see you Monday morning."

"I'll be waiting."

He kissed her and she clung to him, not wanting to let go. She wanted to tell them she'd changed her mind. Instead, she slowly pulled away from Kade, her gaze meeting his as she took a step backwards.

"Be careful," Kade said.

She nodded, spun and hurried in the front door, coming to a stop when she saw Roy leaning against the counter.

He straightened, walking around to open the door that led out of the reception area.

"I thought you told me to learn my own way around here."

"I can go if you want."

Amber shook her head, following him through the corridors, wondering if they had a map of the place. Probably not. That'd make it too easy for their enemies to find their way around if they got hold of it.

A woman stepped out of one of the rooms along the corridor they were in, a sheathed sword hanging at her side. Roy stopped abruptly. "Mum! What are you doing here?"

"Leave us."

"What?" He looked from his mother to Amber. "No. Are you crazy? I shouldn't have told you."

"Of course you should have. Now go to your class."

Amber tensed, wondering if she should call up some fireballs in case she needed to fight her way out of this situation.

Roy shook his head. "I can't. They know I'm bringing her to class."

"Tell them she stopped to use the bathroom and said she could find her way from there."

"No."

"Roy–"

"No." Roy crossed his arms over his chest.

Amber couldn't understand why he was bothering to protect her. His mother had given him the perfect excuse.

His mother stared at him for a moment before she sighed heavily. "You're as stubborn as your father."

"So you keep telling me."

Amber chuckled. "Why do people say that like it's a problem?" She held out her hand to the dark skinned woman. "I'm Amber."

The woman didn't take her hand. "I know who you are."

Roy uncrossed his arms so he could gesture towards his mother. "My mother, Eliza."

Amber continued to hold out her hand. "It's considered polite to shake hands when you meet someone. Unless of course you plan to kill them."

Eliza took her hand, her grip firm. "There's also the chance that a person shakes your hand because they plan to kill you, but don't want you to know."

Amber smiled, mimicking Ronan's predatory one. "Good to know we're on the same page." She drew heat to her hand.

Eliza pulled away from her. "I'll do what is necessary." Her gaze momentarily went to her son before she continued to meet Amber's gaze. "Come with me."

"Where to?"

"No." Roy reached out to place a hand on Amber's arm.

She saw the fear in his eyes. Was he worried for her or himself? Or maybe his mother. "You can come too. I'll need someone to show me where my class is after I've talked to your mother."

Roy pulled his hand back, looking between them. He nodded. "Hurry up or we'll be in trouble for being late."

Eliza strode ahead of them through the corridors. Eventually she stopped, opened a room and stepped in, gesturing for them to enter.

Amber looked around, surprised to find it was the same room where she'd first met Martin. "Why here?"

"No one can hear what happens inside once the door is closed." Eliza shut the door and locked it.

"Now what?" Amber remained ready. If Eliza attacked her she'd fry her. She thought of Paili and how she'd driven the flaming sword into her. And the nightmares that had followed. Maybe she could manage it. "Well?"

"What are your plans?" Eliza demanded.

"My plans?"

"I won't let you harm him."

"Him?" Amber frowned, trying to make sense of the conversation. "Roy?"

"Yes."

"Why would I harm him?"

"She thinks you're going to tell someone. Or blackmail us. We have no family members in Brisbane that are high ranking in the Knights," Roy said.

Amber held up a hand. "Okay, let's start from the beginning." She pointed a finger at Roy. "You told your mum I figured out what you are."

He nodded.

Amber took a step closer to Eliza who held her ground. "And you're here to make sure I don't harm your son." She breathed deep. Impossible. Absolutely impossible. She took another step.

"Don't you come any closer," Eliza warned, her hand resting on the hilt of her sword.

Amber held out her hand. "Give me your hand."

"What for." There was suspicion in Eliza's tone.

Amber didn't blame her. She'd be suspicious too. "He takes after his mother, doesn't he?" She heard Roy's sharp indrawn breath and Eliza took a step backwards. "How?"

"The usual way," Eliza hissed. "My mother was captured by a dragon, but she escaped."

"Surely someone realised."

Eliza shook her head. "I was born late. My mother told her husband I was his. He still doesn't know."

"But what about Roy? Why risk it?"

"I never planned to have him. He was an accident." Eliza's gaze was drawn to her son and her expression softened. "My mother and I went away for a while. I picked a fight with my husband, pretended we were over. I planned to come back after I got rid of Roy. When I saw him-" she broke off, looking away for a moment. "When I saw him, I couldn't do it. He is mine." She met Amber's gaze, her expression fierce. "Mine. I'll do whatever it takes to protect him."

"I'm not going to harm him."

"You will one day."

"Killing me won't help."

"Who've you told?"

"Dragons."

Eliza reached for Roy. "We have to go. Now. Before they kill us."

Roy pulled away from her. "It's a waste of time running. They'll find us eventually."

"I'm not planning to tell anyone," Amber said.

"You already have."

"That was in case something like this happened." It hadn't been, but it sounded plausible.

"If we're going to die anyway, we might as well take you with us." Eliza drew her sword.

Amber lifted her hands, fireballs filling them. "You don't want to do this. Listen. I haven't told anyone else because I need Roy's help." She frantically tried to think of why she needed it. Getting to class wasn't a good enough reason. She needed Rian. He was good at stuff like this. But dragons weren't allowed in the headquarters. She almost grinned. Dragons weren't allowed in the headquarters. Perfect.

"I won't betray the Knights," Roy said.

"I don't want you to. You're the only one here I can count on to look out for me. If something happens to me, my dragons would make sure everyone knows about you. They can't be in this building to protect me, but you can. I don't want you to kill anyone for me, just protect me long enough so I can get away."

"Why didn't you say something sooner?" Roy asked.

"I was going to ask you this weekend. When we were at archery training. I didn't know if there were any listening devices around here."

"Only in the classrooms and dining room," Roy said.

"And her room." Eliza continued to hold onto her sword. "Why would you need someone to protect you?" She nodded towards Amber's hands. "Why can't you protect yourself?"

"I can, if it's only a couple of people. But I seem to have a lot of people putting me on their list of people they'd like to kill this year."

"People?"

"Dragons. But they're not above hiring human assassins."

"So you want my son to throw away his life to protect yours."

"No. I'm hoping an extra person will help even the odds if it becomes necessary. Especially since no one would be expecting me to have allies here."

Eliza lowered her sword. "If he protects you then you'll swear to keep our secret."

"If he lets nothing major happen to me while I'm here, from the moment I arrive, to the moment my dragons collect me, then I'll tell no one here your secret."

"And what about the ones you've already told? Your dragons."

"I can't speak for them, but they have no reason to tell anyone else. I asked them to keep the information confidential unless there was danger to me from the Knights."

Eliza sheathed her sword, holding out her hand.

Amber extinguished the flames and shook her hand.

"If you harm my son, I will hunt you down."

"Fair enough." Amber took Roy's hand that he held out to her. "A deal?"

Roy nodded. "Yes."

"Good. Then let's get to class before we're in trouble."

"Too late, we're going to be in a lot of trouble," Roy muttered.

"Do you want–" Eliza started to say.

"No." Roy unlocked the door. "Go home, Mum. Everything is fine." He stared at her until she nodded, then stepped out of the room.

Amber followed him through the corridors, dropping her bag in her room on the way to their classroom, wishing they didn't all look the same. "Why don't you lot do something to make it easier to figure out what corridor we're in. Hang paintings on the walls or something."

"That'd make it easier for the enemy to find their way around. It's all kept the same to confuse anyone who enters the building. Including keeping the doors shut."

She'd known there had to be another reason other than tidiness. "Why don't you lock the front door if you're worried about people getting in?"

"No need. There's a camera on it and Knights ready to deal with anyone who enters without permission." Roy opened a door, stepping back to let Amber enter first.

Stanley looked over at them, pointing a finger. "You're late. An hour in the training room after dinner. Both of you."

She was tempted to let Roy take the blame too, but that probably wasn't fair. It also wouldn't make him any happier to show her around the place. "Roy was only late because he was waiting for me."

"Do you want two hours? For both of you? Because if you do, keep arguing."

Amber kept her mouth shut, stepping out of the doorway so Roy could enter the room. She'd tried. Maybe he wouldn't blame her. She glanced over at him. It was hard to tell. He didn't look angry or happy.

"Now, as I was saying before we were interrupted," Stanley shot a look towards Amber. "We aren't having archery lessons tomorrow. I was just informed that two Knights from Sydney will be here to do a demonstration followed by one-on-one training. Only the older students will be allowed to train with them and only those not under any punishments."

Maybe she better leave her bed unmade and her clothes scattered everywhere tonight. The last thing she needed was lessons from more Knights. She doubted they'd be any better than the Knights she'd already met.

"All right. Pair up. Time to practice with your swords."

Amber was relieved when it was Roy who faced her, his sword out and ready. At least he didn't try and kill her like Jennifer did. It'd be nice if she could just once disarm him. It wasn't like she was hopeless in battle. It was only that this wasn't her style of fighting. Claws, wings and fire. That was what she was used to in battle.

The lesson passed quickly and Amber began to think she might actually be starting to learn something. Maybe she should get Kade to teach her sword fighting next week. Or even Rian. When Stanley called an end to the lesson, Amber was glad to sheath her sword and follow Roy to the dining room. He let her go ahead of him when she entered the room, following her to her table once she was served.

She was tempted to tell him he didn't need to go to that extreme, but there were too many people who'd hear her. She'd wait until they were at the training room. When they did arrive there and she started to talk to him, he interrupted her.

"I'm not listening."

Jogging beside him, she frowned. Was he telling her to shut up because he didn't want to hear what she had to say or was that his way of telling her there were listening devices in this room too? Was it considered a classroom? Her frown cleared. Why hadn't she thought of it before? He was part dragon. She reached for him with her mind. *"Can they hear us in here?"*

Roy stumbled, sending her a startled glance. *"Yes."*

"You don't have to sit with me."

"Stay out of my head. I don't want you reading my mind."

"I can't. I'm not that good."

"Are you sure? My mum said my mind was like an open book so she couldn't help but read it."

"All I'm getting are the words you're giving me."

There was a long pause before Roy answered her. *"If I'm expected to protect you I need to sit close."*

"Okay."

"Maybe I should put you in a bedroom next to mine in case you're attacked in the night."

He was taking this far too seriously. *"I'll be fine. I can call you like this if I get in trouble."*

"It won't work unless I'm in the same room as you."

"I'll be fine. The whole idea is to make people think I don't have allies here. Then surprise them if they do attack."

Roy nodded slowly, still jogging. *"That's a good tactic. But what happens if you're attacked in your room?"*

"I'll make enough noise that the entire corridor will hear me." She slowed. *"Do we have to jog so fast?"*

"You don't have to keep up with me."

Amber slowed more and Roy pulled ahead of her.

"They say you've killed dragons. Many dragons."

She wanted to ask him who 'they' were. *"No."*

"You haven't killed dragons?"

It probably wasn't a good idea lying to a temporary ally. *"I haven't killed many. Only two."*

He slowed until he was alongside her. *"What was it like?"*

She met his gaze, trying to decipher the look in his eyes. It wasn't the same one Dominic had when he'd learned. There was wariness, maybe even a touch of fear. She shook her head. *"Something I wish I hadn't needed to repeat."*

They fell into silence as they continued to jog, leaving the moment their hour was up. Roy left her at her room, after first checking that no one was in there. She held back her smile until he'd left, grabbing her bag and heading to the bathroom.

Chapter Ten

The next morning when Amber sat at a table in the dining room, not only Roy joined her, but also Dominic. She watched him across the table, wondering what he looked so happy about.

"Why are you suddenly so attached to Amber?" Dominic's eyes were firmly on Roy.

"I told him he needed to show me around." She noticed Stanley was watching them and she wished she'd sat as far from him as possible. At the time it had seemed easier to sit at the empty table, which was right across from Stanley, than have a table become empty when she sat down.

Dominic's gaze travelled to Amber. "I was told to show you around."

She shrugged.

Dominic turned to Roy again. "So you don't need to do it anymore. It's my job."

Roy put his cutlery down and started to speak.

Amber interrupted, worried about what Roy might say. "You didn't want to show me around. You made that very clear when I wouldn't answer your questions. I told Roy he had to do it. I might have even insinuated that my grandfather suggested it."

"So you lied to him."

She shook her head. "Not at all."

"Will you stop answering for me?" Roy sent Amber a look that clearly told her to shut up.

"Fine."

"Do you trust her?" Roy asked Dominic.

"Of course I don't. None of us knows her."

"And yet you thought it was okay for her to wander around our headquarters unaccompanied."

"Oh." Dominic sent a quick look over his shoulder towards Stanley. "I'll show her around from now on."

"You ditched her. I've taken over. Find something else to do." Roy returned to his breakfast.

"This is my job. Dad gave it to me." When Roy continued to eat, Dominic demanded, "Did you hear me?"

"Unless he's deaf he would have heard you." Amber smiled. "Actually, everyone in the dining room probably heard you."

Dominic looked around the room, his expression

growing thunderous. He turned back to Roy, pointing a finger in his direction. "My job. Got it?"

Roy placed his cutlery on his empty plate, rising to his feet. "No." He collected Amber's empty plate and took them to Stanley.

Dominic rose to his feet, planting his hands on the table to lean over it and glare down at her. "We'll see what my father has to say about this." He stalked away, headed for the door.

"Amber, come here."

She looked in Roy's direction, seeing Stanley talking softly to him. Rising from her seat, she hurried to his side. "Are we ready to go yet?"

"We left five minutes early last night." Roy's voice was flat.

"From what?"

Stanley answered her. "The training room."

"No we didn't."

Stanley smiled. "Are you going to argue again? I can give you longer in the training room if you want."

"How long have we got?" She thought of the Knights who were going to be here today. Had Roy been looking forward to training with them? She really hoped not.

"Until lunch. The first hour jog around the track,

the rest of the time use the other equipment. In future complete your full punishment." Stanley continued to smile.

Amber wanted to get rid of his smile so badly. Her hands curled into fists as she fought the urge to form fireballs. She hadn't wanted to see any other Knights. But he didn't know that and he was doing this deliberately. Relaxing her hands, she dredged up a smile of her own. "I probably should be thanking you. The gym equipment is much easier to use than a sword." Her smile widened when Stanley's vanished. Turning on her heel, she strode towards the door.

"He'll think of something else to get back at you," Roy warned her.

"What's his problem?"

"His parents were killed by dragons when he was five."

"Oh. I didn't know."

"He argued against you being here."

Pulling out her phone, Amber sent a text first to Kade and then to Ronan to let them know she wasn't going to archery today. She probably should have done it last night, but she hadn't wanted to deal with Ronan's questions. When Ronan's reply came through, she nearly laughed. He was so predictable sometimes. She quickly answered his why with the fact that two Knights from Sydney were arriving today to give extra training. She didn't bother telling him she wouldn't be a part of it. That would only lead to more questions.

They arrived at the training room as Amber returned her phone to her pocket, starting to jog slowly around the outside. This time Roy kept pace with her. Several times she checked her phone, wishing the hour would pass quicker. Saturday's weren't meant to be spent stuck inside jogging around a track, being punished for something you hadn't done. It was mid October. The beach would be perfect this time of year. Not too hot, but certainly warm enough for swimming. And she was stuck here doing circles because someone hated dragons and was taking it out on her. It wasn't right.

Getting on the exercise bike once the first hour was over didn't improve her temper. She sent text messages to Crystal while she half-heartedly pedalled, complaining about how much it sucked here. When Crystal said she'd ring, Amber told her there was no point since there were listening devices in the training room as well as the other classrooms and her bedroom.

When she'd finished chatting to Crystal, she read a book on her phone, staying on the exercise bike. About every half an hour she noticed Roy move onto a different piece of equipment, but she didn't bother. The exercise bike seemed the easiest and at least she could do other things while she was on it to help with her boredom.

It was nearly lunchtime when a scent caught her attention and she looked in the direction of the door, seeing two dark skinned men just inside the training room. She returned her phone to her pocket, keeping a wary eye on them. *"Roy? Who are they?"*

"The visiting Knights."

She hopped off the exercise bike, walking towards them. She heard Roy's footsteps behind her, but didn't turn to look. Stopping out of arm's reach, she stood, arms crossed as she returned their stares. They were both a similar height with hazel eyes, dark brown hair closely cropped, swords at their sides and a similar look to them that made Amber think they were related. She breathed in deeply, frowning. "You're Knights?"

"My uncles." Roy stood beside her. *"Remember the listening devices."*

She nodded. "Your mother's brothers?"

The two men turned abruptly without answering and left the training room, headed down the corridor. *"They want us to follow,"* Roy told her.

"They spoke to you? In your mind?"

"Yeah. I told them you could hear mind talk, but they didn't want you to read their minds."

"I can't do that."

"I told them, but they don't believe you."

Amber walked beside Roy. The two men remained ahead of them. They eventually arrived at the room Roy's mother had taken her to, closing and locking the door once everyone was inside. One of them remained at the door, arms crossed, feet firmly planted as he watched her.

"I thought Eliza said your mother escaped. How did she end up with three kids?" Amber moved to a spot in the room where she could see all of them, wishing they could have stayed next to each other to make the task easier.

"How do you know?" The one standing in front of the door asked.

It was frustrating not knowing who she was talking to. Nearly as frustrating as not knowing what was going on. "Doesn't anyone believe in introductions anymore?"

Roy pointed to his uncle who stood in front of the door. "Isaac." Then he pointed to the one pacing the room. "Amos."

"How do you know what we are?" Isaac asked again.

"I can smell it in your blood."

"How?"

She shrugged, not sure how to answer Isaac's question. "Any dragon could."

"You're not a dragon."

"No."

"Then how?" There was an edge to Isaac's voice this time.

"I don't know. I just can. Like I can smell the dragon bone on all the other Knights and in the food each time it's added. I can smell poison and sometimes even fear." She felt the panther in her half-heartedly try to escape at the word fear. She pushed it back down. No one was afraid at the moment. There was no prey for it to chase.

"Why can't the Knights smell it? Why can't we smell it?"

"You probably could. But I have no idea how dragon bone works, so I don't know how well Knights can smell."

Amos stopped his pacing. "There are too many other smells. Unless one is extremely overpowering they all blend."

She shrugged. "Guess you'll have to figure it out for yourselves."

Amos crossed the room, stopping in front of

Amber so she had to tilt her head back to meet his gaze. "Tell me."

She breathed in deep, smelling the dragon. It was a stronger scent than it had been on Shylah. She had no idea what that meant, unless he was about to change form. "You change into a dragon and I will attack you. Now back off." Amos glanced towards his brother then took several steps away from her. She wondered what Isaac had said to him. Whatever it was, it didn't look like he appreciated it.

"Why won't you tell us? What else are you hiding?" Isaac asked.

"Probably just as much as you're hiding." She glanced at Roy who moved to sit on the edge of the table. "How about you tell me how come there's three of you. Eliza said her mother escaped. Are you triplets?"

Isaac stared at her for several minutes before he spoke. "I answer that and you tell me how you can smell dragon in the blood."

Amber nodded. It probably wouldn't help him much, but that wasn't her problem.

"The dragon thought it was amusing that our mother passed Eliza off as the daughter of a Knight when she's half dragon. He captured her again. We're twins."

Amber's stomach lurched. It sounded so much like something Ronan would do. "Do you know his name?"

"Tahmid." Amos spat the name out, his lips twisting into a sneer. "If I ever find him, I'll kill him."

Amber swore, taking an involuntary step back before she forced the shock from her face.

Isaac crossed the room in a blur, a dagger in his hand, holding it against her throat.

Amber called fireballs up, pressing one to his arm, pulling away the moment his grip loosened. She backed away, her hands up, warily watching the three part-dragons who stood in front of her. Two with swords drawn, one with a dagger. "You won't all live."

"I'll turn dragon and then we'll see who lives," Amos said.

"She's killed two dragons." Roy lowered his sword. "Even if you killed her, they'd still find out."

"But at least we'd take her with us." Amos took a step towards her.

She looked at each of them, trying to figure out the best plan. Roy she wasn't certain of. He didn't have the look of someone about to kill her, but that didn't mean anything. If his uncle's attacked she doubted he'd defend her against them. "Your enemy is my enemy."

Amos laughed. A sharp, harsh sound full of disbelief. "I doubt it."

"He wants the secrets I know. He's already killed one of my allies and gained some of them."

"What secrets?" Isaac demanded.

"How to make Dragon Mages." Silence filled the room and Amber began to wonder if she should speak again. She had no idea what to say and didn't want to make things worse.

"You still owe us an answer." Isaac pointed at her with his dagger.

At least that would buy her some time while she tried to think what to do. "You need to focus on one of the scents. Block out the others."

"How?"

She shrugged. "I'm not sure. I found it easier to do when I was hungry. When I was learning to control the panther. The dragons taught me to follow the scent. Pull it to me."

"You've got your answer, Isaac. Now we can kill her."

"Surely you've got other questions." Amber extinguished the fire in her hands, pulling her shirt off to reveal the dragon-leather vest she wore underneath. She dropped it on the ground.

"What are you planning?" Isaac demanded.

"No more than you're planning." She barely managed to speak the words when Amos attacked. Throwing a fireball at his chest, she leapt into the air, turning into a goshawk and streaking across the room.

Chapter Eleven

Isaac chased her, throwing his dagger and drawing his sword.

Amber dodged the dagger, hearing it embed itself in the wall as she faced them, becoming human long enough to throw more fireballs at them. As soon as she became a goshawk, she flew across the room out of Isaac and Amos' reach.

"Stop! All of you stop."

They ignored Roy, continuing to attack. Amber flew past Amos, coming up behind Isaac to turn human. Drawing her sword she stabbed it through his side, leaping out of the way when his legs gave out and his knees collided with the ground.

Amos roared, running towards her, slashing with his sword.

Amber turned into a goshawk again, flying out of the way.

Roy ran to his uncle, screaming. "Stop it. Heal him. Please heal him." He pulled the sword from Isaac, letting it fall to the ground.

Amber landed on the table, turning human. "A life for a life. I heal him you owe me my life."

"He's dying. I can feel it," Amos snarled. "You can't change that. Death is final."

"Promise me." She pointed at Amos. "You promise me. If I save him you will never attack me ever again. Or have someone else attack me. No matter what happens you owe me that."

Amos lowered his sword. "He dies so do you."

"Hurry." Roy cradled his uncle on his lap, blood staining him and the floor.

"Promise me." Amber held Amos' gaze, willing him to hurry before he caused her to be responsible for another life. "Now. Before it's too late." She could hear Isaac's heart slowing.

"I promise."

Amber jumped off the table, rushing past Amos to kneel at Isaac's side. She pressed her hands against his wound, seeking the dragon in him. He was weak, had lost too much blood, but she could do this. Power poured through her hands and she healed the wound, working from the inside out. Exhaustion swamped her and she wrapped a bloody hand around one of her bracelets, drawing power from it.

Isaac's hazel eyes opened and he met hers. "Why?" The word was barely a whisper.

She reached for his mind. *"You were trying to kill me."*

"No. Why heal me?"

"Because I have more than enough blood soaked nightmares without letting you give me more."

He reached up, brushing his fingers across her cheek and jaw. *"You're not what I expected."*

Amber grinned. *"I get that all the time."*

"What's going on?" Amos knelt across from Amber, resting his hand on his brother's shoulder. "I can still feel how weak he is."

"Of course he's weak. Look how much blood he lost."

"He'll live?" Roy pressed a hand against his uncle's heart. "He's not going to die?"

"No, but someone might if we don't have a good reason for the mess we made in here." She could just imagine what Stanley would do. Probably blame it all on her and demand her death.

Isaac grinned. "We wanted to test your skill. We'd heard so much about you."

"You're not going to tell them she won." Amos made it a statement, not a question.

Amber laughed. They were very much dragons. "It was a tie." Her grin remained in place. "Obviously."

"It wouldn't have been if you hadn't cheated." Amos glared at her.

"Killing someone isn't cheating." Isaac tried to sit up. "Help me up, why don't you? And quit bitching at me. You're giving me a headache. It could just as easily have been you."

Amber rose to her feet. "I didn't stab him because I knew he'd be too pig headed to forgive me. That's why I made him be the one to promise not to attack me."

Roy laughed, a startled sound that he cut off before it had barely begun. "She knows you already."

Amos glared at Roy and Isaac who both grinned. "We'll get this cleaned up. You two go to lunch." He eyed them. "After you've showered and changed."

There was a sharp knock on the door. Amos and Amber swore at the same time and Amos sent her a look as if to ask how dare she be even the slightest bit like him.

The handle rattled.

"Are we going to open it?" Roy asked.

"You open it." Amos collected his sword while Roy crossed the room.

Amber grabbed her shirt and picked up her own sword, grimacing at the blood on the blade. Her gaze was drawn to the door as Roy swung it open. When she saw Charles and Martin in the doorway she grinned. "Well isn't this just perfect."

"What's going on?" Martin drew his sword as he entered the room.

"No one is meant to harm her." Charles left his sword at his side. "Do you know how many dragons they'll have here if she dies? We can't get that many Knights organised quick enough to protect ourselves."

"We were training," Amber said.

"It was a tie," Amos quickly added.

"You're unharmed?" Charles eyed her up and down. "Whose blood?"

"Mine," Isaac and Roy said together.

"Both of you?" Martin asked.

"Probably a little bit of everyone's," Amber said. "It was a tie after all."

Martin's gaze narrowed in on Amber. "Did you start this?"

"I wanted to know what a mage can do," Isaac said.

"What did you discover?" Charles asked.

Isaac met Amber's gaze and held it. He smiled. "That she can hold her own in a fight."

She nodded, returning his smile.

"Everything is all right? We aren't going to have two castles full of dragon warriors turning up on our doorstep?" Martin demanded.

"Everything is fine," Amber said.

"Then get to class." Martin glanced at Roy. "Both of you."

Her stomach growled. "What about lunch?"

"You missed it," Martin said.

"I doubt it. Not unless you want a panther roaming your corridors."

"Go get cleaned up and we'll meet you in the dining room," Isaac said.

"You aren't the High Protector here, Isaac. I don't come into your headquarters and start throwing my weight around," Martin said.

Amber barely managed to control her shock. She reached for Isaac's mind. *"You're High Protector?"*

He sent her a grin, ignoring Martin. "Twenty minutes. I'll organise someone to prepare lunch and get this place cleaned up." He strode from the room, Amos on his heels.

Charles grabbed Amber's arm when she started to

walk past him to follow Roy. "Are you certain you're unharmed? There's a lot of blood in here."

"I'm fine." She met his sharp blue eyes, holding his gaze. She was confused, trying to figure out what the hell was going on, but physically unharmed. "Was that all?"

Charles let her go.

Amber held his gaze a moment longer before she strode after Roy, who had stopped partway along the corridor. He showed her to her room and as soon as he'd gone, she grabbed her bag and headed for the bathroom. Standing under the warm spray of the shower, after she'd cleaned her sword, she tried to figure out what was going on. Obviously Roy had lied when he'd said his family wasn't important. She tried to think of what he'd said. 'We have no family members in Brisbane that are high ranking in the Knights.'

She chuckled. Typical dragon. No, but they were here now and they were a very high rank. What had she been told about the Knights? She frowned. Sydney. Headquarters were in capital cities. Isaac was the High Protector of New South Wales. How had he managed that? He was half dragon. And why had he managed that? Just because he wanted to kill his father didn't mean he had no ties with other dragons.

Ronan would want to use this information and she couldn't keep it from him. Not without losing all the ground she'd gained with him. Turning off the shower, she reached for her towel, stopping centimetres from it, swearing. They could be Golds. Whatever the headquarters were made of they didn't keep dragons out, only prevented them from remaining in the Void. How many other Knights had dragon heritage? Her hand closed around the towel, drawing it to herself. Why did everything have to be so complicated? Dragons always had to make things far more complicated than they needed to be.

She pulled on fresh dragon-leathers, bundling up the bloody ones and putting them in the plastic bag she carried for her laundry. Kade was not going to be impressed when he learned about the fight. Neither was Ronan. She thought about his threat to get her bodyguards. Human ex-military ones. That was the last thing she needed.

Returning to her room she found Roy leaning against the corridor wall, arms crossed as he waited for her. She ditched her bag in the wardrobe and followed him to the dining room. Isaac and Amos were already there, four plates of food on the table.

Amber sat across from Isaac, Roy across from Amos. She inhaled the scent of food, noticing no dragon bone on any of the meals. Smiling, she began to eat.

"What's so amusing?" Isaac asked.

Amber shook her head, remembering the listening devices. "Nothing." Then directly to Isaac, *"How have you managed to avoid dragon bone your entire life?"*

"I haven't. The weakness doesn't last forever. Up to a month. Usually only two weeks."

"Just like how long the effects last when you consume dragon blood?"

Isaac nodded then glanced towards his brother. *"Amos wants to know what is going on."*

Amber reached for each of their minds. *"Is that better? Can everyone hear now?"*

"Get out of my head." Amos glared across the table at her.

"I can't read your mind. I'm not good at that. Some dragons can, but they have to actually make the effort. Although there is a constant buzz behind your words. Maybe you're kind of broadcasting."

"You can read my mind."

"No. If I tried I probably could, but I'm not trying. It's more than enough effort keeping you all connected. Normally someone else does that when I'm in a group and we're talking together." She hesitated, knowing her next

words were going to cause problems. *"I have to tell my allies."*

Amos rose to his feet, his hand going for the hilt of his sword before he dropped it. *"You did that deliberately. I can't fight you. I can't stop you from telling anyone."*

"Sit down, Amos." Isaac continued to eat.

Amos remained standing. *"We'll lose everything. Including our lives and you're going to sit there calmly eating your food?"*

"I'm going to eat my lunch while I listen to what she has to say. I suggest you do the same."

"Why? So I can die with a full stomach? How's that going to make death any less final?"

"There is only one of my allies who will want to use the information. I will ask him to keep the knowledge to himself, but I can't promise anything. Especially if it will benefit him," Amber said.

"Then why tell him?" Isaac asked.

"Because she wants us to die." Amos dropped into his seat, his food remaining untouched.

"Because he's my ally and I share what I learn with him."

"Does he do the same?"

Amber smiled at Isaac's question, almost laughing. *"No, but in exchange he protects me."*

"Who is your ally?" Amos demanded.

Chapter Twelve

Amber really wished he hadn't asked her. No one ever liked the answer. *"Ronan."*

Roy groaned. *"We're dead. All of us."*

Amos leapt to his feet again. *"You tricked me."*

"Sit down, Amos." Isaac stared up at his brother, waiting until he sat. He turned to Amber. *"Are you certain he's your ally?"*

She nodded, her smile widening. *"Absolutely."*

"How did you manage that?" Isaac asked.

She glanced towards Amos. *"Maybe I tricked him too."*

Isaac shook his head. *"No. He's far too smart to be tricked."*

"Or far too confident to have much faith in a mere human to survive long enough to become his ally."

"You actually tricked Ronan?"

She shrugged at Isaac's question. *"I'm still trying to figure that out. Maybe we tricked each other. It's complicated."* Like far too many other things in her life because of dragons.

"We need to meet with him," Isaac said.

She had no idea how she could do that without all hell breaking loose. *"I'll see what I can arrange."*

"We'll arrange it," Amos said.

"Good luck with that. No one arranges Ronan."

The dining room door opened and Dominic entered. His gaze darted to Amber before resting on Isaac. "Stanley sent me to look for you. To see if you need me to show you where his classroom is."

Isaac rose to his feet, pushing his empty plate away from himself. "We know where to find it. You clean up the plates, Dominic." His gaze travelled to the table. "Lunch is over. Time to train." He strode for the door.

Amber turned away from the angry look Dominic sent her as she followed Isaac and Amos, Roy beside her. She was going to have to keep an eye on Dominic. He might not be her enemy yet, but with the rate she was gaining them lately there was a good chance he'd eventually become one.

As soon as they entered the classroom, Stanley strode across the room, his gaze boring into Amber.

"You're late. You and Roy to the training room. Stay there until dinner."

Isaac stepped between them. "They were with us. I wanted to meet the mage."

Stanley remained quiet for a moment. "You should have sent word. She's a disrespectful student that believes she can do as she pleases. Been with dragons too long and learned their undisciplined ways."

Amber fought the urge to defend dragons, trying to remind herself that he had good reason to hate them. It didn't help. She still wanted to argue his words.

Isaac nodded. "My apologies." He strode to the front of the classroom. "Everyone pair up."

Amber moved closer to Roy when Jennifer looked in her direction. *"Is this normal? High Protectors teaching."* She sent the words to Roy only.

"Yeah. And other high ranked Knights. It's so all students get as much training as possible."

"High ranked. Are they not high ranked when they're in Brisbane?"

Roy flashed her a grin. *"They weren't in Brisbane at the time."*

"That is such a dragon comment." Roy looked away and Amber regretted her words. *"That wasn't an insult. It was probably closer to a compliment."*

Isaac stopped in front of them. "Do you two need a personal invite to start?"

Amber looked around and saw that everyone else was mimicking the movements of Amos and Stanley's mock battle. Their weapons didn't touch, moving away at the last moment. How the hell did they expect her to be able to do that? She drew her sword and tried to follow the movements.

When Isaac called a halt and sent everyone to one end of the room to stand along the wall, she was grateful. That was until Isaac explained they each had to take turns against Amos. She met Amos' gaze when he looked at her, letting him be the one to look away first when Josephine joined him in the middle of the room, sword drawn.

Josephine lasted about ten minutes. Only Roy lasted longer than her, nearly twelve minutes. Even Dominic, when he returned, didn't last that long. Then Isaac called Amber and she strode to the centre of the room, her sword out. She'd begun to think they weren't going to call her, instead they'd left her for last.

Amos dropped his gaze to her legs before meeting her gaze again. "Do you have another one of those dragon-leather vests on under your shirt to match those trousers?"

"Yes."

"Then take your shirt off and put away your sword. Fight me with your skills, not ours."

"Why?"

"Because I've seen how you fight with a sword. I'm not having anyone believe I was tied against someone who fights like that."

Amber grinned, sheathing her sword, pulling off her shirt to toss it towards Roy. She was surprised when he actually caught it. She'd half expected him to let it fall on the floor. "Rules?"

"Anything goes."

Amber raised her hands, fireballs pooling in them. "Are you sure?"

His lips slowly curved into a smile. "Bring it on."

She flung the fireballs at him, spinning to the side as he dodged and slashed at her with his sword. Another two fireballs followed the first two, barely missing him. His sword came towards her and she knew she wouldn't be able to get out of the way in time. Becoming a goshawk she darted past him, raking her claws across his cheek as she went. Coming up behind him, she turned human, her hand brushing his back as she dodged his spinning attack.

"Lucky I didn't have a dagger." She jumped up, changing form to fly above the sword that slashed through the air where she'd been. Landing to become human again.

"It would have barely been a graze." Again he attacked.

She dodged. "I guess that's two strikes for me." She nodded towards his cheek, warily watching him as he edged to the side, his sword motionless for now. Then he came at her with a flurry of attacks and she took flight, coming up behind him, dodging the swinging movements of his sword. Clawing his other cheek before she landed at the side of him in human form. "Three strikes. Does that make it my fight?"

"Not even close." He attacked again, this time cutting her arm.

The scent of her own blood filled the air and when she tried to turn into a goshawk to dodge again, the panther forced it's way through and she tackled Amos, his sword flying across the room. Her teeth were around his throat before she could stop herself. The room was filled with yelling, bringing her back to her senses. She let go of his neck, becoming human again, crouched over him. "My fight?"

Amos laughed, pushing her to the side so he could rise, holding out his hand, a dagger in it. "If it had been a real fight it would have been a tie."

Amber rose to her feet, grinning. "Again? I guess

we're too evenly matched." She pressed a hand to her arm, healing the wound. "Want me to heal yours?"

"You said you can't heal Knights," Josephine said from where she stood near the far wall.

"I might have figured a way." Amber held up her hand. "By using my blood." She turned to Amos. "Well?"

He shrugged. *"You better be right about this. If they learn I'm a dragon my brother will kill you."*

She pressed her bloodstained hand against his cheek. *"And your sister too, I'm sure."* Reaching for the dragon in him she healed the claw marks she'd caused. She stepped back, lowering her hand.

Amos nodded. "Thanks." He looked around the room. "You all did well. I expect to see even more improvement the next time I'm here." He looked in his brother's direction and as one they headed for the door.

Roy crossed the room, handing her the shirt she'd thrown at him. "You outlasted all of us."

Amber pulled her shirt on, wondering how many more of her clothes would end up bloodstained this weekend. "I've been in several battles, Roy."

"You didn't lose." He gestured to the rest of the class. "We didn't even get close to a tie."

"Maybe he should have let each of you choose your own fighting style."

"The sword is our fighting style. Against you a sword is useless."

She met Roy's gaze seeing the concern in their depths. She didn't know what to tell him, then wondered why she should even want to reassure him.

"I'd like to see her try and survive a gun," Jennifer said.

Amber faced her. "Didn't you already see that?" She paused. "Ah no, that's right. You and your father were too busy being overpowered by a single dragon in human form."

Jennifer raised her fists, starting forward. "Why you-"

"Jennifer!" Stanley's voice roared through the room. "Back in line. Now."

She glared at Stanley for a moment before she took a step back. The look she sent to Amber promised retribution.

"You two." Stanley pointed to Amber and Roy. "In line. Class isn't over yet."

Stepping into line, Amber wondered how many of the class hated her. Certainly Jennifer, possibly Dominic. She wasn't sure about Roy. Holding something over someone could be dangerous. But what else could she do? Kill him because she'd found out his secret and he might want to kill her to keep her quiet? She couldn't do it. Killing in battle was hard enough.

Stanley made them pair up and do more sword drills before he let them go. When Amber and Roy would have followed the rest of the class out the door he called them back. "An hour in the training room."

Amber opened her mouth to protest.

Roy grabbed her arm, tugging her towards the door. "Okay, Stanley."

When they were in the corridor, Amber pulled away from him. "We didn't do anything."

"So? You want to stand in there and argue with him and miss dinner?"

"Yes. Well, not miss dinner, but–"

"Come on. You're wasting your breath."

She stared after him, anger making her want to go back in and deal with Stanley. When Roy glanced over his shoulder she sighed, hurrying after him. It wasn't fair. They hadn't done anything wrong. Once they reached the training room she was tempted to sit down and watch Roy jog, but joined him, her pace slower than last time. While she jogged, she sent a text to both Ronan and Kade to let them know she was fine. Then several to Crystal to complain about how much she hated being here. There was still more time to waste before she could leave so she sent a few messages to Angela who she hadn't chatted to in ages. When Angela had to go have dinner, Amber checked the time and nearly groaned. There was still fifteen minutes.

Ahead of them, the door swung open and Isaac and Amos stepped into the room. Isaac stood with his arms crossed waiting, while Amos came to meet them.

"What are you two doing in here? Do you live here or something? We've been looking for you for ages."

"Circumstances," Roy said.

Amber snorted.

Amos walked beside them. "If you've got something to say, then say it."

"Stanley sent us here after class." She sent the words to all of them, then thought she better say something for anyone who might be listening. "We're just so dedicated to training we spend every moment we can in here."

"Why?" Amos demanded.

"It doesn't matter," Roy said.

At the same time Amber said, *"My fault."*

"What did you do?"

She smiled at Amos' question. *"Became involved with dragons."*

Isaac uncrossed his arms when they reached him. "You're coming to dinner with us. No time to finish your punishment tonight. You'll have to do the rest of it in the morning."

"Dinner? Where?" Should she warn them that she'd have dragons following her? At least two of them.

"Does it matter?" Amos asked.

"Yeah. I have to let Ronan know where I'll be. He'll get annoyed if I take off without telling him." And she wasn't stupid enough to go somewhere unknown with possible enemies.

"That's good. We want to meet him. Somewhere private. Without anyone knowing," Isaac said. "Give him a call."

"I'll need to speak to him. Out the front." She wasn't going to text that to him and obviously they didn't want her to say it out loud where the information could be heard.

"We'll wait inside while you talk to him." Isaac led the way.

Chapter Thirteen

Amber sent Ronan a text while she walked. It didn't take long for a reply to come. *This better be good.* She smiled. It was right up his alley. Plenty of intrigue and who knew what hidden agendas.

Ronan stepped out of the Void when she arrived out the front, staying well away from the front door. "What's going on?"

"I have three Knights who need to speak with you privately. And no matter what you learn you have to let them return here afterwards. Alive. And you have to keep their secrets. At least for now."

"Knowledge is power, but it loses its power if it can't be used."

"Give them a year."

"Why should I?"

She thought of several reasons, but discarded each of them. *"Because they're the enemy of your enemy."*

"Which one?"

She slowly shook her head, a slight smile forming. *"I should have known you'd need a name. Most people have only one, if any."*

"I don't have all night."

"Tahmid."

"Will this knowledge help us take him down?"

"I'm sure you'll be able to think of a way to use it without telling anyone the information."

Ronan stared at her for several minutes before he nodded. *"Call them out. I'll organise my Golds to take them to my place."*

"And they'll be safe?"

"If they don't attack me, I won't attack them. They'll be safe for tonight." He looked away from her. "Chait, Alsandair. Out of the Void."

Kade stepped out of the Void too. "What's happening?"

"What are you doing here? Aren't my Golds good enough to look after her?"

"You haven't been here all weekend have you?" Amber asked before an argument could start.

"Of course not." Kade crossed the space between them, sliding an arm around her. "Rian has a gold watching the place. He came and told me when Ronan appeared."

She shook her head. "This is overkill."

"Go and get your Knights," Ronan said.

She looked around at the group gathered in front of her. "This actually works out better. Kade, you can take Roy." Her gaze fell on Ronan. "Where are we taking them?"

"My water garden."

With a nod, Amber drew away from Kade and headed back inside. She stopped, barely in the door when she saw that Martin, Dominic and Charles were now waiting with Isaac, Amos and Roy. She bit back the words that first came to mind, pretty certain they wouldn't answer her demands of what they were all doing there. "Are we having a party?"

"Everyone wants to go to dinner," Isaac said.

"Impossible. Ronan–"

Martin interrupted Amber. "We all go or none go."

Amber's hands went to her hips. How dare they try and interfere? It took her only seconds to come up with a plan. She checked first that the door was closed behind her. It was. "I spent all that time convincing Ronan that no one wants to harm me. That this dinner isn't some diabolical plan to get me away from his warriors. The only way he'll let you have dinner with me is if you join him at his house."

"Then you arrange for all of us to go," Martin said.

"I was barely able to convince him to let three join him."

"Then you'll have to cancel," Martin said.

"And have him wonder what you'd planned to do? If they don't go after I got them safe passage for the night it'll look like they wanted to get me alone and harm me."

"They need to go," Charles said. "You don't want to give Ronan an excuse to attack."

"It's safe to go with him?" Roy asked.

"I'll go if you're too afraid," Dominic said.

"There should be a representative of the Queensland branch," Martin said. "Roy can stay and Dominic will go in his place."

"Are you saying Roy doesn't belong here?" Isaac demanded.

"He's your nephew. That would make him loyal to the New South Wales branch. Just because your sister and her husband chose to move to Brisbane doesn't mean they've cut ties to their original branch," Martin said.

"Ronan won't accept that. I told him it was a family

dinner I was invited to. Dominic doesn't look like he's related at all."

"Since when do Knights feel loyalty to only their local branch, or even their state branch? We are Knights. We should be loyal to the entire organisation," Charles said.

Amber glanced behind her at the closed door. "You better hurry up. They'll wonder what's taking us so long."

"Go," Martin snapped.

Amber pushed the door open, holding it so Isaac, Amos and Roy could step through. Grabbing Roy's arm, she strode towards Kade. "Take Roy." Letting him go, she stepped up to Ronan. "Let's go."

Ronan's gaze travelled to each of the Knights before stopping on Amber. "You've got a lot of explaining to do, kitten."

Amber grinned. Before she could say anything, Ronan took her arm and they went through the Void to his water garden. When everyone had arrived she made introductions. Her words were greeted with silence. "I hope that once you've all finished glaring at each other that we're going to have dinner. I'm getting hungry and the excuse we used was going out to dinner. I'm pretty sure they'd be asking all sorts of uncomfortable questions if I came back hungry."

"Chait, take their phones." Ronan waved him forward.

"Why?" Isaac asked.

"So you don't use any locating app to find this place. Now hand them over if you're not planning anything like that." Ronan waved Chait forward again.

Isaac was the first to hand over his phone, followed by Roy and Amos. "How do we know you're not going to do something to them?"

Amber stepped in front of Chait. "I'll take them."

"They need to be turned off first," Ronan said.

"Why should we trust you not to do anything to them either?" Amos demanded.

"Who would you prefer to have them? Me or Ronan?"

Amos glared at her for a moment before he replied. "You."

She took the phones after Chait had turned them off, not certain what to do with all of them. Keeping them in her hand, she asked Ronan, "Are you organising dinner?"

"Would I let you starve, kitten?"

"Only if it benefited you."

Ronan chuckled. "A good thing for you that there's no benefit to it at the moment." He sobered, his gaze going to Isaac. "How did dragons infiltrate the Knights?"

"Tahmid is their father."

Ronan's head turned quickly towards Amber. "You better start at the beginning and don't leave anything out."

She did, with interruptions from both Isaac and Amos. When Ronan continued to stare at her, she asked, "What?"

"Does he have anything to do with you?" Ronan directed his question to the brothers.

Isaac answered. "No."

"This could be useful."

"How?" Amos asked Ronan.

Ronan smiled, looking like a predator who was within reach of an elusive prey. "I'll let you know when I have all the details sorted."

"Why should we be interested?' Amos demanded.

"You want Tahmid dead, don't you?"

Amos nodded.

"Then I'll let you know when you can help. For now," Ronan gestured towards the entrance to the house. "Dinner is served."

"How do we know it's safe to eat?" Amos asked.

"The meal hasn't been dished up and the plates and

cutlery are still in a pile on the table," Ronan said. "But most importantly, I gave my word."

"We don't even know what the time is," Isaac said.

Amber checked her phone. "It's nearly ten. No wonder the panther is complaining."

"Still the same day," Isaac said.

Ronan chuckled. "Yes, you're safe until midnight. Not everyone pays attention to the little details. That must be the dragon in you."

"I prefer to think it's the Knight," Isaac said.

Ronan shrugged. "This way." He led the way to his dining room, letting them all help themselves to the food.

It was well after eleven when the meal ended and Isaac, who had been regularly asking Amber the time, said they needed to leave. Amber reached for Kade's hand. His fingers tightened on hers.

"Can't we stay a little longer? There's still time before it's the next day," Amber said.

Isaac shook his head. "Time to go."

When they all rose from the table, Kade drew her to his side. "I'll see you Monday morning."

"That feels like a decade away," Amber muttered. She pulled away from him. "Take Roy." As soon as he nodded, she crossed the room to Ronan, letting him take hold of her arm to return her to the Knights' headquarters. Amber gave them back their phones the moment they arrived.

Ronan faced Isaac and Amos. "If anything happens to her while your nephew is guarding her I'll hold you personally responsible."

"The harm won't come from us," Isaac assured him.

"He better protect her from anyone who would harm her or you'll wish for death." Ronan disappeared back into the Void, Chait and Alsandair disappearing too.

Amber threw her arms around Kade, kissing him, her fingers threading through his hair. She drew back slightly, her gaze meeting his. "Angela was asking me about schoolies. You interested in going to it with me?"

"Are you crazy?" Roy asked. "You can't invite a dragon to schoolies."

"Feasting and celebrating. Sounds like just the place to invite a dragon." Kade smiled. "It's a date."

She stared up at him, the word date ringing in her head. They'd never had one. Nothing had been normal about their relationship. Not one single thing. "Okay." She let go of him. "I'll see you Monday." She followed the Knights inside, stopping when she saw her grandfather was waiting for her. What did he want now? She came to a halt in front of him, Roy stopping not far from them.

"Go on, Roy. I'll show her to her room."

"Will you be okay?" Roy asked Amber.

She started to nod then stopped when she realised it'd look odd. "I'll see you in the morning."

Charles waited until they were alone before he spoke. "Are you unharmed?"

She nodded.

"What happened tonight?"

"We had dinner."

"You were gone a long time."

She shrugged. "Ronan can be entertaining when he wants to be."

"Is there anything I should know?"

Amber laughed. A sharp sound filled with disbelief. "You're kidding me, right? Do you seriously think I'd share anything with you? How many times have you and Grandma threatened to kill me? I'm only here because we made a deal. I've tried giving your Knights a chance, but they're not interested. Roy and his uncles are the ones that have been the nicest to me, which isn't saying much since their only interest in me is to find out how easy it is to kill a mage."

"Are you saying something happened tonight?"

"I'm saying that's a stupid question to ask. In future

don't bother with it. The answer will always be no, even if there's something to be shared."

"While you're here you'll abide by our rules."

"I never agreed to that. While I'm here all I have to do is give the Knights a chance and not attack anyone unprovoked." A pity she hadn't told Roy to wait in the corridor for her. "Are you going to show me to my room?"

"When I'm ready."

"Forget it. I'll find my own way." She opened the door behind the counter, ignoring her grandfather calling out to her. Heading down the corridor she was relieved to see Roy waited for her at the end of it. He pushed away from the wall as she reached his side. "Didn't I tell you I'd see you in the morning?"

"You didn't answer my question."

Amber smiled. He'd asked her if she'd be okay. "I guess not."

He silently led her through the corridors, leaving her at her door. Amber watched him head to his own room. She didn't have a clue if he was a friend or enemy and she hated not knowing. Yawning, she got ready for bed. Morning would arrive far too quickly and there'd be no sleeping in. They still had to finish up in the training room.

Chapter Fourteen

Monday morning Amber followed Roy to the exit, glad to be going home again. Even though yesterday had been uneventful, she'd still had to put up with Stanley. She pitied the Knights who didn't seem to have any breaks. They trained seven days a week.

"When do you have time off?"

"We get holidays."

"When?"

"At set intervals." Roy opened the door to the reception room, staying in the corridor. "I'll see you Tuesday afternoon."

She started to ask him her question again, then nodded. What did it matter? She wasn't about to become a Knight. "Okay. See you Tuesday arve." She crossed the reception room and stepped outside, glad to see Kade emerge from the Void under the shadowy branches of the fig tree. She hurried towards him, wrapping her arms around him.

When they came out of the Void onto his verandah, they were kissing and Cooper cleared his throat to get their attention. Amber reluctantly pulled away. "What?"

"Why can I smell blood?"

Kade frowned. "Dried blood. What happened?"

She tossed her bag to Cooper. "Make yourself useful. See if you can get blood out of dragon-leather."

Cooper caught the bag. "Are you hurt?"

"It's not my blood."

"Whose is it?" Kade demanded.

"Give me a break. I just got home. Can we talk about it later?" It was the last thing she wanted to discuss after having spent an entire weekend with the Knights. She just wanted to forget all about them for a bit.

"You were hurt, weren't you?"

At the anger in Kade's voice, Cooper yelped and scurried inside.

"Of course I wasn't."

"Then why won't you tell me?"

"Because it's complicated."

"We've got time."

Amber shook her head. "No we don't. We've got school."

"Then you better hurry up and tell me or we'll be late."

She could see he wasn't going to relent. Sighing, she slowly shook her head. "Damn dragon."

"I'm waiting."

"You have to remember this happened before Amos promised not to kill me. And you're not to retaliate. I nearly killed Isaac."

"Why would I want to retaliate if you were the one who nearly killed them?"

"Because I didn't start it. And before you go thinking I should have told you at Ronan's, I didn't want to tell you while we were with the Knights." She quickly explained what had happened, knowing she was going to have to retell it to Ronan again later. When she finished, she sent Ronan a text telling him that when she had time after school she'd tell him the full story of how she'd ended up bringing Isaac and Amos to dinner.

She read the text he sent back. *Don't bother. Alsandair just arrived to tell me all about it.*

He better get it right. When no reply came back, she put her phone away. Damn dragons interfering all the time. "Ready to go?"

Kade nodded as Maira and Brann came out of the house. On the way to school Amber told them about her training fight.

"Did he get the dagger out before you had his throat?"

She shook her head. "I don't think so."

"Then it wasn't a tie."

Amber grinned. "Let him have his tie. I know how much you dragons hate to lose."

Maira chuckled. "Some more than others." She parked out the front of the school and everyone clambered out, heading to their classes.

Amber was relieved school was uneventful that week. Keeping up with both school and Knight's training was becoming exhausting. She probably shouldn't have asked Kade and Rian to start teaching her to use a sword each morning, but she needed to learn. It was a matter of life and death. By the time Friday afternoon came around she hadn't improved much, but Rian had given her a sword of her own and she had returned his.

When Amber reluctantly drew away from Kade and headed inside the headquarters, she found Roy waiting for her. He silently led her to her room where she could dump her bag and Amber wondered if there was a problem. The walk to class was equally quiet. Afterwards, the walk to the dining room and then to her room were also silent.

"Roy?"

About to walk away, he turned back to her.

"Is everything okay?"

"Yeah."

"Are you certain?"

"What do you want me to tell you? I think it's awesome you hold our lives in your hands? That I think Ronan is going to keep quiet? It's only a matter of time. No matter what I do one of you will eventually get us killed."

"I'm sorry. I don't have any plans to harm you or your family, but I can't promise you that your secret will always be safe."

"That's what I thought." He strode away.

"It won't necessarily be Ronan or me who lets the secret escape."

He kept walking.

Amber watched until he entered his room before she stepped into her own. It wasn't a good start to the weekend. She thought the same thing again when he walked with her to class the next morning. Silently.

They were about an hour into the lesson when Amber's phone rang. She answered, ignoring the glare from Stanley. He'd been the one to ask to have her in his class. His problem if he didn't like the results. "What's wrong, Mum? Can't it wait until Monday morning when I'm out of this dump?"

"Amber."

Fear skittered through her at the whispered wail. "Mum? Where are you? What's wrong?"

"He has a gun."

"Who-"

A man cut off her words. "I want you, Cooper and Miles. And I want the three of you here within the hour or I'll be using this gun."

Why didn't he have Miles? Shouldn't he be with her mother? "I don't have Miles. I wouldn't have a clue where he is. I haven't seen him in ages."

"Then you and Cooper and you better have some information on Miles that we can use to find him."

"Who are you?" Amber strode towards the classroom door, ignoring Stanley who called her back.

"It doesn't matter. One hour. You and the boy."

The phone went dead and Amber stared at it, trying to keep calm.

"Get back here now. Class isn't over. You won't get any special treatment in here just because of whose granddaughter you are."

Amber spun, pointing a finger at Stanley. "Shut up.

My mother is being held at gunpoint by a dragon."
A murmur went around the classroom. Amber strode
for the door, opening it as she rang Ronan. She
stopped in the corridor, not sure which direction to
take.

Roy came out of the room and silently led the way
when she told him she needed to go to her room.

Ronan answered the phone. "Have they broken the
rules?"

"No. I need–" she stopped her plea for his help. She
had to think clearer. Panicking wasn't going to save
her mother. "A dragon is holding my mum hostage.
At gunpoint. He wants Cooper and me. Do you
think it's Tahmid?"

"I doubt it. Probably one of his warriors."

"Is Chait and Alsandair still out the front?" She
continued to follow Roy through the corridors
towards her room.

"Yes. But don't you even think about handing
yourself over. You still owe me."

"No, I don't. You were the one who asked for my
help, not the other way around."

"In payment for the favours you owed me."

"What you want is worth way more than two
minor favours. I'll see you out the front of the

headquarters in a few minutes. This will go a little way towards making things even between us."

"Nice try, Amber. This'll make us even. Don't be long."

Amber slid her phone into her pocket as she reached her room. Inside she pulled off her shirt, replacing the skimpy dragon-leather top with a dragon-leather vest. She was already wearing dragon-leather trousers. She threw her door open, running into Charles who came to a stop in front of her.

"Leaving will break our agreement."

Amber glanced behind Charles to see Martin and Helen coming along the corridor, several metres behind him. Roy still waited for her. "Mum is being held by a dragon, at gunpoint."

"I doubt it very much." Martin stopped beside Charles. "Didn't you say she has nothing to do with the dragons?"

"He wants me in exchange for her. Now out of my way." She tried to push past them, but Martin grabbed hold of her arm.

"Are you certain?" Helen demanded.

"Of course I'm certain." Amber tried to pull her arm out of Martin's grip. "Let go of me now. You call yourself a Knight and yet you're about to let an innocent human be killed by a dragon."

"Let her go, Martin," Charles ordered. He turned to Amber. "Don't leave without us. Hel and I are coming too."

"If you're not ready, I'll be gone." Amber turned to Roy. "Run. I'll keep up with you." Even if she had to turn into a panther to do it. She followed Roy, pulling her phone out again and dialling Kade's number.

"I heard. Ronan told me. I'm on my way."

"Thank you."

"Don't do anything stupid until I get there."

Amber laughed, an abrupt sound that was lacking humour. "Does that mean I can do something stupid when you arrive?"

Kade chuckled. "Yeah. Then I can help you with it."

"Okay." About to say goodbye, she remembered her grandfather's order. "My grandparents are coming too."

Kade swore. "We really need to get more of our own Golds. We can't keep relying on Ronan."

"I'm going with you," Roy said.

She started to argue then decided that another Knight, even one still in training, might be a good idea. "We've got one more Knight coming with us," Amber said.

"Who?"

"Roy. I'll see you shortly." Amber hung up as she reached the reception area, her gaze drawn to Dominic, his hand resting on the hilt of the sword hanging at his side.

"I want to come with you."

She shook her head. "No way. You treat me like I'm contagious and then you expect me to let you fight at my side when you ask. I doubt it. I wouldn't trust you not to stab me in the back."

"You were the one treating me like I was contagious." Dominic pointed to Roy. "Are you taking him with you?"

"I don't have time for this." Crossing the room, she opened the door, stepping outside, Roy following.

Dominic grabbed her arm. "Amber–"

Ronan stepped out of the Void. "Let her go boy or I'll tear your arms off."

Dominic let her go to draw his sword. "A dragon?"

"Put your weapon away. He's with me." Amber stepped in front of Dominic.

"But, I heard you. On the phone. You're going to kill dragons." Dominic lowered his sword his gaze going from Amber to Ronan.

"I'm not planning on killing anyone."

Ronan laughed. "Don't we know it, kitten. Yet how many dragons have you killed so far?"

Alsandair stepped out of the Void. "I hear it's two." He came closer to Amber. "Want me to take you to your mother?"

She wanted to protest that she hadn't been the only one to kill Queran, but she didn't. She had been the one to decide that he'd needed to die. "Kade can take me to Mum."

"Then why isn't he here?"

"Two dragons?" Dominic sounded confused. "They're dragons."

Chait stepped out of the Void. "Three dragons, little Knight." He grinned.

Kade joined him. "Four."

Amber began to worry there'd be a fight. "Go inside, Dominic. We don't need your help and we wouldn't trust you anyway."

"But you'll trust him." Again Dominic pointed to Roy. "Or has he changed sides and is helping the dragons."

Roy started to speak, but Martin, Charles and Helen came out the front door. Martin grabbed Dominic by the arm, pushing him towards the entrance. "Get inside and put that away. What are you trying to do? Have someone call the police?"

Dominic sheathed his sword. "I want to go too."

"Inside." Martin's tone cut off any arguments. As soon as Dominic left, he turned to Ronan. "I'm going with you."

Ronan laughed. "That's as likely as me taking your son. You might as well go inside with him."

"We don't have time for this. We have to save Mum."

Ronan nodded. "Your grandparents and the boy? Any others, Amber?"

"I've already said-"

Amber cut off Martin. "No others."

Ronan grabbed her arm and took her through the Void to his water garden.

Amber pulled away from him. "What are we doing here? My mum is in danger."

Chapter Fifteen

The rest appeared out of the Void, including Anrai, one of Ronan's Golds, bringing Cooper with him. Anrai held onto Cooper tightly while he begged to be left alone.

"Cooper. Cooper!" Amber was about to shout his name again when he stopped babbling and faced her. "They've got my mum."

"What about Miles?"

Amber shrugged. She didn't know where the other Dragon Mage, who had been made at the same time as Cooper, was. Nor did she know if they had her mother's boyfriend Gary, who also lived with her. "They want you and me in exchange for her."

"You're going to give me to them?" His voice grew high pitched.

"I'm getting my mum back. If that means you and I

going in there and letting them think we'll exchange ourselves for her, then that's what we're going to do."

"They'll kill me. They said they'd kill me if I didn't come willingly." Cooper tried to break free from Anrai.

"Shut him up," Ronan ordered.

Anrai knocked Cooper out, letting him collapse onto the ground.

Amber opened her mouth to yell at Ronan, then closed it when she saw his amused expression. She didn't have time for this. "We need to go right now."

"Not without figuring out a plan." Charles pointed a finger at her. "If you get my daughter killed I will kill you."

"She's my mother. I'm not about to get her killed."

"Chait. Give the Knights some of your blood so we can communicate with them." Ronan sent a look to Roy. "All the Knights."

Roy took a step backwards away from a dragon Amber didn't recognise, shaking his head. "I'm not having anyone's blood."

Amber said directly to Roy, *"Don't fight him on this. It gives you a reason to be able to hear the conversations in our minds and he's also letting his dragons know that you're a Knight, not the dragon you smell like. They'll think you're one of his people, which is safer for you."*

Then aloud, "Take the blood or be sent back to the Knights' headquarters."

Roy nodded.

"You haven't had any dragon bone in the past week, have you? They can make you sick if you have them too close together," Charles said.

Roy shook his head.

"Make sure you leave it at least a week before you have any more dragon bone," Charles said.

"If you're all finished?" Ronan continued when they remained silent, "Kade will take Amber. Anrai will carry Cooper. The rest of us will stay in the Void until we're needed. No one else is to come out of the Void unless I do. Turi." A gold stepped out of the Void. "You will take the young Knight."

"Who will you take?" Amber asked.

Ronan smiled. "Your mother."

She nodded. "Then let's do this." She held out her hand to Kade. He took her to her mother's front yard, coming out of the Void on the concrete footpath leading to the front door of the lowset, unpainted, besser block house. The place wasn't much to look at, but it had a solid two metre high fence all around it and all the neighbours had lowset houses. Which made it perfect for coming unnoticed out of the Void.

Anrai came out of the Void next to them, Cooper thrown over his shoulder.

"Be careful." Kade tightened his grip on her hand before he let go and vanished into the Void.

Amber stared at the open door of her mother's home. "I'm here."

"Come inside and get your Gold to step out of the Void."

"Kade." He stepped out when she called his name and she began to wonder why they hadn't thought to call Crystal. There could be dragons in the Void all around them.

"Come inside," the man ordered again.

Amber led the group, scanning the area as she slowly walked up the path, Anrai behind her, Kade following him. When she stepped inside, she blinked, trying to adjust her eyes to the dimness of the lounge room. Her mother sat in a chair that had been brought out of the kitchen, a dragon standing beside her, a gun in his hand. The rest of the lounge room looked untouched. If there'd been a fight, someone had cleaned up. "Who are you?"

The man laughed. "Gethin. Not that it'll matter. You don't know me, but I've heard all about you." He pointed the gun in her direction.

"Who sent you?" Amber asked. She reached out

checking for others in the house. It was empty. Where was Gary and Miles? They could be anywhere. What if Tahmid had Gary and why did no one know where Miles was?

Gethin laughed again. "Do you really think I'm about to tell you that?" He gestured towards Cooper who Anrai still carried over his shoulder. "Is that Cooper?"

Amber nodded.

"Looks like he didn't want to come with you."

Amber nodded again. What were they supposed to do? How quickly could she cross the room? Could she reach Gethin before he turned the gun on her mother?

"You!" He aimed the gun at Anrai. "Put the mage down over there and you can sit on the ground near him, your hands on the carpet where I can see them." He gestured to the place with his gun. "And you too." This time he pointed the gun at Kade.

Amber tensed, watching the gun as it was casually pointed around the room. What was she supposed to do? "Are you okay, Mum? He didn't hurt you?"

Donna nodded then shook her head.

"Anyone else hurt?"

Again Donna shook her head. "They weren't-"

"Shut up." Gethin pointed the gun at Donna.

Amber's breath caught in her throat. "You've got Cooper. And me. Let her go."

"I don't think so." He continued to hold the gun on Donna. "I never said anything about letting her go. Only that I'd shoot her if you weren't here in time."

"Then what's the point? If you don't let her go she's still in danger and probably dead. I'm not about to stay and let you take out the two of us." She took a step forward. "What would be the point?" Another step. There was no way she was going to let him kill her mother.

The gun swung in her direction. "Don't move. He said not to kill you. Nothing was said about not harming you."

The moment the gun was on her, Amber flew at him, turning into a goshawk in mid leap. The gun went off and she felt the bullet fly past her. Then she was landing behind him, drawing her sword and plunging it into his back. Blood gushed over her hands. Her mother stared at her, mouth open. She didn't have a clue where Ronan was, but she wasn't about to wait for him to get her mother to safety. "Anrai! Take Cooper out of here. Kade, take Mum."

Chaos erupted. Knights and dragons poured out of the Void, not all of them allies. Amber didn't have time to think about the dragon dying at her feet.

Another one attacked her, his sword swinging fiercely. She ducked, sheathed her sword and become a goshawk to dash out of the way. She came up behind him, but he was ready for her, spinning to face her as she landed and turned human. Dodging out of the way, this time she became a panther, leaping on him and going for the throat. These dragons had threatened her mother. They'd held a gun at her head and terrified her. Mind numbing rage filled Amber and she launched herself at a man who was attacking Kade, who'd returned, roaring as she landed on him.

The battle became a blur of friend and foe. Torn out throats, bodies littering the ground and blood. An ocean of blood. Snarling, Amber turned on the person who touched her. Shock filled her when she realised it was Kade and he was saying her name over and over again in her mind.

She forced the panther away, finally becoming human. Kade's hand rested on her shoulder and she wiped her mouth on her arm, leaving a smear of blood behind. There was blood on her hands and she could taste it. A metallic flavour that made her want to throw up. Everywhere she looked she could see blood. Panic hit her. *"Get me out of here. Now!"* She spoke directly to Kade.

With a nod, he took her through the Void to his bedroom, wrapping his arms around her.

"How many?"

"How many what?"

Amber drew away from him. "How many did I kill?"

He shook his head. "I don't know."

She began to tremble. "They had my mum." Tears filled her eyes and she held them back, her throat aching. "They were going to shoot her."

Kade reached for her again. "Survival of the fittest."

Amber stepped backwards, out of his reach. "No. I'm not a killer. I'm not." The last words were softer. Broken.

"They threatened your family." Again he reached for her.

She let his arms wrap around her, sliding her own arms around his waist. "I need a shower." She could still taste the blood in her mouth. "How many did I kill?" She spun, pulling away from Kade as she felt someone enter the room from the Void. Her hands dropped when she saw it was Ronan.

"You can't imagine how proud I am of you, kitten. Well, I was until I found you in here sobbing about the lives you took. You were magnificent. If I had of known that all it took to bring the dragon out in you was to hold a gun on your mother I would have done it months ago."

Guilt was instantly replaced by a fierce protectiveness and she stepped forward to jab a finger at Ronan's chest. "Don't even think about it." Her words were low and threatening.

"Are you sure you won't reconsider mating with one of my sons? What about Rian? With his level headedness and your fierceness my grandchildren would be invincible."

"No." Amber and Kade spoke at the same time.

Ronan shrugged. "It was worth a try. Maybe one day you'll say yes."

"Why are you here, Ronan?"

"Your mother is having hysterics and after the way you fought for her I thought it was probably not a good idea to deal with her the same way I dealt with Cooper."

"Where is she?"

"My place. Everyone's there. Including Gary and Miles who were at his office."

Amber turned to Kade. "Take me there."

"Are you sure you don't want a shower first?"

She looked at her bloodstained hands. She could also feel blood on her face. "Ronan, tell her I'll be there shortly." Flinging open the bedroom door, she strode towards the bathroom.

"I'm not a messenger boy," Ronan called after her.

She ignored him and guessed he left through the Void because she could no longer feel him in the house. When she returned to the bedroom after having a shower, she found dragon-leather trousers and a vest laid out on the bed for her. Mentally searching for Kade she found him in the lounge room. As soon as she was dressed, she headed there.

Kade rose from an armchair. "Are you ready to go?"

She nodded when all she really wanted to do was go somewhere else and try and forget this day had ever happened. An image of her tearing someone's throat out came to mind and she quickly pushed it away. "Yeah."

They arrived at the water garden to find Anrai waiting for them. He showed them to the lounge room where everyone was. Amber heard them long before she reached the room. Charles and Ronan were fighting. She stopped in the doorway, not wanting to deal with more problems.

She felt someone watching and looked over to see Roy staring at her. *"What's wrong?"* She began to think he wouldn't answer her.

"You killed six."

A shudder went through her. *"I couldn't have."* The battle hadn't lasted that long. Surely there'd only been two, maybe three.

"I saw you. You killed six."

Amber swallowed hard, her stomach somersaulting like it was about to empty its contents. She thought of all the blood on her mouth when she'd become human and wondered how much of it she'd swallowed. Her stomach flipped again and she took a deep, shuddering breath. It didn't help. The scent of blood still on everyone else both repulsed and drew her, making the panther want to escape.

She held Roy's gaze. *"They threatened my mum."*

He nodded. *"I'd do the same for my family."*

"Are you going to stand there all day, kitten?"

Amber looked towards Ronan. "No."

"What were you doing?"

"Talking to Roy."

"Don't worry, Roy, it'll wear off in a couple of weeks. Four at the most," Charles said.

"What were you talking about?" Ronan asked.

She couldn't bring herself to say.

"Her kill count," Roy said.

Amber tried not to wince.

"It was six," Ronan said.

Roy met Amber's gaze. "I told you."

Ronan laughed. "Guess that makes it eight now, kitten." He smiled at her, a mixture of pride in his predatory smile.

Amber felt uncomfortable, especially with her mother listening to the conversation. She came into the room. "What were you arguing about?"

Chapter Sixteen

"He wants to keep Donna here," Helen said.

"We all know what his hospitality is like," Charles said.

Amber shook her head. "No. She'll go to Temolae Keep." A thought struck her. "Has anyone warned Jay and Crystal? And what about my dad? Do they know about him?"

"I sent Golds to watch each of them," Ronan said.

Kade was right. They really needed to get more of their own Golds. They relied on Ronan far too much. She turned to her grandfather. "Today hasn't changed our deal any."

"What deal?" Donna demanded.

"To spend time with the Knights."

"Is that what they've been teaching you? How to fight? I saw you before Kade took me out of there.

You killed that man. Stabbed him in the back like he didn't matter."

Anger hit her. She'd saved her mother's life and now she was in trouble? How wrong was that? "He was going to kill you. What was I supposed to do? Let him?"

Donna shook her head. "No, but…" Her voice trailed off.

Amber crossed the room, stopping in front of her mother who was seated in an armchair. "It was him or us. Would you have preferred he killed me?"

"No!" Donna rose to her feet. Her hands reached for Amber's shoulders. "No. I don't want anyone to kill you and I don't want you to have to kill anyone. You're a child. This isn't right."

Amber smiled at the irony. "I think the phrase is it's not fair."

"When did you stop being my little girl?"

The pain in her mother's voice made her ache. She'd had longer to get used to it all than her mother had. "I didn't, Mum." She closed the distance between them, giving her mother a fierce hug before stepping away.

"Something certainly changed."

"Yeah, it's called growing up." She faced Ronan.

"Did any of the enemy survive?" She again pushed the image of blood from her mind.

"Not a single one." Ronan's smile still had a touch of fatherly pride in it.

Amber nodded. "Have your Golds take my family and the two mages to my castle. Then return the Knights to their headquarters."

"Are you giving me orders, kitten?"

Amber smiled, slowly walking towards him. "Are you saying my suggestions don't make sense?"

"They sounded like orders to me."

"We're not leaving until we know what's going on," Charles said.

"I'm not leaving until I know you're safe," Donna said to Amber.

"I'll see you after school on Monday, Mum." She turned to Charles and Helen. "I'll be back at the headquarters within the hour. I need to make sure everything and everyone is secure."

"This is our business too," Charles said.

Amber shook her head. "No. It isn't."

Helen gestured towards Donna. "She's our daughter. Whatever you're up to, put her in danger."

"I'm not up to anything other than being sick of always being the target." Amber tried to take a deep calming breath, but it was going to take more than that to feel calm. Especially with the scent of blood in the room. "So you can stop blaming me for everything that goes wrong."

Anrai picked Cooper up off the floor, swinging him over his shoulder and disappearing into the Void. Chait grabbed Miles and Alsandair took hold of Gary. They all vanished.

Amber looked at Ronan, a question in her expression. When he nodded, she nodded also.

"Let me go." Donna tried to pull away from Chait who had returned already. It didn't help. She vanished into the Void.

"Don't think you're going to take us out of here like that," Charles said.

Ronan grinned. "You're welcome to stay if you want. Your room is still prepared."

Chait, Anrai and Alsandair reappeared, each standing next to a Knight. Amber held up a hand. "Wait." When no one moved, she continued. "I won't be long. Even if you stayed you wouldn't be able to hear what was going on. So you might as well go."

Charles pointed a warning finger at her. "If you're more than an hour you owe us an extra day."

She nodded, letting her hand fall to her side. The three dragons took that as a signal to take the Knights through the Void. Amber turned to Ronan. "What now?"

"We wait."

"For what?"

Ronan shrugged. "Things."

"He's still waiting for you to help him take out Tahmid and support him in claiming a Council seat," Kade said.

"So this hasn't changed anything?" Amber demanded.

"Of course it's changed things. I need to get you a pair of daggers. That move of yours, coming up behind them like that, was inspiring. It'd work much better with a pair of daggers."

Amber felt like growling. "Be serious, Ronan."

He crossed the space between them. "I'm always serious when it comes to survival."

She felt Kade come closer, but kept her gaze on Ronan's, catching a flash of gold in the depths. *"They're all going to find out soon, aren't they? You're going to stop hiding what you are."*

Ronan nodded. *"The time is coming. I will take their warrior sword and step up onto their dais and all will see I am Gold. No one will be able to argue the fact since it's impossible for anyone but Gold to hold the sword. Then things will change."*

Amber felt fear skitter through her. She didn't want things to change. *"What changes? You planning on trying to rule the world?"*

"No. Dealing with things that should have been dealt with back when I was a boy. This change would come with or without me. This way we'll be prepared and we will win."

"What changes?"

"In time, kitten. In time." His gaze went over her shoulder to Kade. "You can go now."

Amber was tempted to argue, but she knew Ronan. He kept his plans to himself. Never sharing them until the last minute. She stepped backwards, feeling the warmth of Kade's chest against her back. His arms went around her waist. "Take me to your place, Kade." Ronan's gaze remained on her until they vanished.

When they arrived in Kade's room, she remained in his arms, turning to face him, sliding her arms around his neck as she looked up at him. "I don't want to go back." Even with her eyes open she could still see the blood. She dreaded to think what the night would bring.

"Charles will make you stay an extra day."

She remained silent for a moment. "Is everyone safe? All my family?"

"Rian and Maira will make sure of it. We'll get more Golds. Whatever it takes."

She looked into his eyes seeing determination in the golden brown. A fierceness rushed through her and she clasped her hands at the back of his neck. "You too. Make sure you're safe too."

He lowered his head, his lips meeting hers. When he finally drew away, he smiled. "You too."

She nodded then hesitated. The hour must be getting close to over. "Take me back."

Kade took them through the Void coming out in the shadows of the fig tree out the front of the Knights' headquarters. He kissed her one last time before he let her go.

Amber took a step backwards, her gaze still on his. One more step. *"I love you."* She smiled at his raised brow. She knew the question he asked. *"You're mine."* She spun striding towards the front door, his laughter following her.

"You're mine too, Amber."

Her smile vanished as she stepped inside to find Charles and Roy waiting for her.

Charles checked his watch. "Barely."

She bit back the caustic reply that came to mind. "Did you want something?"

"What did Ronan want?"

Amber laughed. "Haven't we already had this conversation?" Crossing the room, she spoke to Roy. "I'm starved. Take me to the dining room. I need lunch." Especially since it was well past lunchtime.

"I haven't finished talking to you."

Reaching the door, she opened it, looking back over her shoulder, laughter gone. "I told you not to bother with stupid questions." She stepped through the doorway, walking beside Roy. After he'd glanced at her for probably the tenth time, she demanded, "What?"

"Huh?"

"You keep looking at me like I'm some strange creature from outer space or something."

"Is it all an act?"

"You're really going to have to be a little clearer." She wasn't in the mood for cryptic conversations.

"In class you're hopeless. A first year Knight could kill you. But I saw you today. You're a warrior. Changing shape, killing, never there when their sword pierces the spot where you'd just been. I saw a bit of it when you fought my uncles, but today…" his voice trailed off and he shook his head. "Today you were invincible."

"They threatened my mum."

"I was beginning to think you weren't a killer.

That Isaac was a fluke. But you are. You tore through that house."

She wished people would stop calling her that. It wasn't true. "I'm not a killer. They threatened my mum."

Roy stopped walking and faced her, a door at his back. "So what are you then?"

She stared at him a moment then smiled, almost laughing when Roy took a step back, running into the door. "Protective." When he continued to stand there, she spoke again. "Don't threaten what's mine and I won't have to turn protective."

"You saved me." He shook his head slowly, his gaze not leaving hers. "I can see you don't even remember it. Two of them attacked me. I parried one, another sword was coming for me. I had no chance to block it. Then you were there, tearing his throat out. Why?"

He was right. She didn't recall it. All she remembered was the blood. An ocean of blood. He continued to wait for her to speak and she tried to think of something to say. "In that battle, we were allies."

"Are we now?"

"I don't know. You tell me."

"If we are, then Dominic might be right. I am a traitor."

He turned and opened the door, walking into the dining room.

Amber followed him, glancing around the empty room, the word traitor ringing in her mind. She sat at the table Roy gestured towards while he went behind the counter and made them sandwiches. They ate silently and Roy cleaned up before he led Amber to their classroom. They found a note from Stanley.

Ripping it off the door, Amber crumpled it up. "I'm getting sick of the training room."

Roy grabbed the paper from her when she started to throw it. "I would have thought you'd be happy to miss archery." He headed along the corridor.

Amber walked beside him. "I'd rather go home and forget about all of this."

When they reached the training room, she got on the exercise bike since Stanley hadn't specified anything in particular. Pulling out her phone she sent a message to Rian, asking how her mother was.

I have removed her phone from her because she kept threatening to call the police. She is demanding that I take her to you.

She momentarily closed her eyes, not wanting to even think about any more problems.

"Are you okay," Roy asked.

She looked over at him. He was doing chin-ups. "Yeah. Mum is being difficult."

Roy grinned. "I know what that's like."

Amber reluctantly smiled. She guessed he did. Looking down at her phone, she tried to think of a reply. *Tell her I'll see her Monday afternoon and she has to stay there to keep us both safe.* No more messages came from Rian and she hoped he had it all under control. If anyone could calm her mother down, it was Rian.

When dinnertime finally arrived, Roy led her to the dining room where they had a table to themselves. Again she reminded him he didn't need to sit with her and again he ignored her. She was glad when they'd finished eating and she could retreat to her room. It had been far too long a day and she was sick of the looks the other kids were sending her and the whispered conversations they thought she couldn't hear. One day they'd be the killer they kept calling her, but they'd be seeking out what they killed. She'd only ever killed those who had tried to turn her into their prey. She had no idea how they'd heard about the fight. Maybe someone had overheard Charles or Helen talking about it. She doubted Roy would have said anything. Not with how concerned he was that he might be a traitor.

Lying in her bed that night, she tossed and turned, trying to sleep. And when it came, blood filled her dreams. She tried to save her family, tried to save her friends, but they were washed away in a sea of blood. She woke gasping, holding back a scream, fireballs in her hands, Roy backing away, his hand still outstretched.

"It's okay."

She extinguished one of the fireballs, keeping one to see by. *"What are you doing here?"*

"Isaac told me to watch over you tonight. You sounded like you were having a bad dream."

"What did I say?"

"Nothing. Your breathing changed and you were thrashing about. They wouldn't have heard anything out of the ordinary."

She remembered telling Isaac she had more than enough blood soaked nightmares without him giving her more. *"Why did he tell you that?"*

"I told him about today. I couldn't sleep so I rang him. Before he hung up he said I should watch over you tonight."

"Thank you."

"Go back to sleep. I'll stay here."

"I couldn't sleep now."

"I haven't been able to sleep either."

She stared at him in the glow of her fireball. Maybe physically exhausting herself might help. *"Is there somewhere we can train?"*

Roy nodded.

She remembered what Ronan had said. *"Are there any daggers around here I can borrow?"*

"I've got a pair in my room." He led the way.

Amber waited at the door for him to get them from his wardrobe. Her gaze travelled the room, surprised at how unlived in it looked. Roy handed her the daggers, handle first, before leading her to their classroom, turning on the light. She blinked as her eyes grew accustomed to the brightness. Extinguishing the fireball, she put a dagger in each hand. When Roy removed a dagger from his boot, she grinned. How many daggers did one person need?

Hours passed as they trained, exhaustion dragging at Amber. When she finally thought she might be able to sleep, she noticed the door was slightly open and Charles stood in the hallway watching them. She met his gaze as she returned the daggers and followed Roy from the room. He didn't speak to her and she didn't speak to him. Halfway down the corridor, she looked over her shoulder to find Charles continued to watch her. She had no idea what he was thinking and was too tired to care. Ronan would probably call her an idiot and tell her she always needed to know what the enemy was thinking, but she was tired. Sick of battle, tired of always looking over her shoulder and exhausted from lack of sleep. Maybe when she woke up she might care again. Although she doubted it.

Chapter Seventeen

She still felt tired when Friday arrived again and she sat in the car beside Kade, school over for the day. It had been the week from hell and it wasn't over yet. Monday afternoon she'd had to listen to a lecture from her mother and had been expected to see her every day after Knight training that week. Cooper had complained about how she kept endangering him and letting Ronan knock him out, but at least he wasn't ringing or sending her text messages every other minute. Tuesday afternoon she'd gone straight from school to Feralenzi to collect Topaz, the dragon egg her and her brother shared the care of, leaving her with him. The only good thing about going to the headquarters this afternoon was that she had the perfect excuse not to visit her mother for another lecture. She had a feeling the lecture would have been a lot more fun.

Closing her eyes, she leaned against Kade. She'd had nightmares every night since the previous battle. The last thing she wanted to do was go running to Ronan again. She had to get over this herself. It was a weakness that would lessen her in his eyes and that she wouldn't allow. She shouldn't be having nightmares. Hadn't she won? Hadn't she saved her mother and made sure all her family were heavily protected? She'd even saved Roy. And yet she was still having nightmares about losing them.

She continued to sit there with her eyes closed when the car stopped and Maira and Brann both got out.

"Are you planning to get out of the car any time soon?"

"No."

Kade laughed softly. "I'm sure you'll get hungry eventually."

About to reply, she felt Ronan step out of the Void nearby and opening her eyes, she reached for Kade. Pressing her lips against his, she hoped that Ronan would believe this was the reason they hadn't got out of the car. She heard the door swing open and Kade tried to draw away from her. *It's only Ronan. Ignore him.*

"Nice try, kitten. Get out here and tell me what's going on."

Amber kissed Kade one more time before she pulled away and smiled at Ronan. "Surely you're not that old that you've forgotten what a kiss is."

"Now."

Amber started to get out of the car, but Kade grabbed her hand, tugging her back to him. His gaze clashed with hers. *"Next time you kiss me don't do it because you're trying to throw Ronan off the scent. Not unless your life is in danger."*

When she nodded, he let go of her hand and she hopped out of the car to stand in front of Ronan.

He looked her over. "We're going to my place."

"I have to pack my bag and go to the Knights' headquarters."

"Kade can organise your bag and meet us at my place." Ronan looked towards Kade who now stood beside Amber. "Thirty minutes." When Kade nodded, Ronan took Amber's hand and transported her to his water garden. "What's going on? You didn't look this bad Tuesday when we collected Topaz."

She smiled wryly. "Makeup."

"You still haven't answered me. What is going on?"

"You keep trying to turn me into something I'm not!"

"And what is that?"

"A killer!" She couldn't stop shouting at him even though she knew she shouldn't.

"A warrior." Ronan grabbed her shoulder, meeting her gaze. He sent her a picture of her landing behind Gethin, drawing her sword and stabbing him through the back, giving orders with her next breath.

"That's not me."

"No? Are you sure?"

"If I'm so great a warrior why do I keep having these nightmares?"

"You'll get over them."

"And then what? I become the killer you're trying to make me?"

Ronan shook his head. "No, then you become the powerful warrior I know you are."

She wanted to protest that she wasn't powerful, but this was Ronan. How many times could she be weak in front of him before he became disgusted in her and left her to try and survive on her own? She knew she could find him, but would she be able to find him in time if he left her to her fate. "Where you see a warrior, I see a killer."

"What do you see when you look at me?"

She laughed, shaking her head, surprised she even knew how to laugh anymore. "I really hope you're not expecting me to want to be like you."

"What do you see, kitten? A killer? Is that what you see when you look at me?"

She sobered, meeting his gaze, seeing gold in the depths of his eyes. A gold that remained instead of disappearing in a flash like it normally did. "Yes, but I also see a warrior. There's strength, a strong will and a determination to survive against all odds."

Ronan smiled. "Too late, kitten. You're already like me."

She pulled away from him. "No!"

He advanced on her. "You think you have different motivations. You care only for your friends and family."

She stopped retreating, holding her ground. "What do you care for?"

"Getting that Council seat."

"And that's it? You only care about yourself? You said that I think I have different motivations from you. I know I do."

"One day soon I might even tell you a story that you'll wish you'd never heard. A story no one else alive knows. A handful know bits and pieces, but not the complete truth."

Did she really need any more fodder for her nightmares? A story she'd wish she'd never heard sounded like nightmare material. "Don't bother. I don't want to hear it."

"You will. You'll be begging me for details. But for now all you need to know is, like everyone else, you only care about yourself. It's what it all boils down to for everyone. Deep down it's how it would make you feel to lose those you love. We all only care about ourselves. About our lives and those entwined in our lives."

Amber shook her head, wanting to argue, but not knowing what words would work. She felt Kade arrive and wanted to run to him, wanted to beg him to tell her she cared about more than herself.

"If you're having nightmares again then come to me. You won't be any use to me if you can't focus when it comes time to kill Tahmid."

"They wouldn't let you stay at the headquarters."

"I would figure something out."

She fell silent a moment as she tried to think, but she was so tired. "Monday night. If they're not gone by then, I'll call you."

Ronan nodded.

She started to turn away.

"Amber."

She faced him again. "What?"

He raised a hand and Alsandair stepped out of the Void, carrying a wooden box. He opened it and Ronan removed two daggers, holding them out to her.

She took one of them. It was about fifteen centimetres long, light and strong, dragon-leather wrapped around the handle. "Why so short?"

Ronan held out two pieces of dragon-leather with buckles. "They go at the wrist. They'll change with you. There's dragon-leather running through them as well as on the handles. This will work better than the sword you use."

Strapping the sheaths on, she slid the daggers in, surprised at how comfortable they were. "Thank you."

Ronan nodded once. "If you leave now you'll be on time and the Knights won't be trying to get another day out of you."

She turned to Kade, holding out her hand. When he took it, they entered the Void, coming out in front of the headquarters. Her fingers tightened on his before she could bring herself to let go and take the bag he held out to her. The last thing she wanted to do was to spend one more moment here.

"Only three weekends left." Kade stepped close so he could kiss her goodbye.

When she finally drew away she smiled. It would be a relief not to have to come back. "And then only one week left of school. Can we go to Temolae Keep or do we have to stay in town until the end of the year?"

"We can spend some time at our castle, but we can't leave town completely. Now go before the Knights are coming out here demanding what's taking you so long."

She hurried towards the door, her hand reaching out to open it. There was an explosion. Smoke filled the air and she heard a car race towards her. Shots were fired and she dropped her bag on the ground as she tried to see through the smoke, coughing. An arm slid around her and a cloth was pressed over her mouth.

"Amber!" Kade called out her name, several other voices echoing him.

She struggled to escape, feeling herself being dragged away, sleep trying to claim her. The last thing she heard was Kade calling her name and another gunshot before the world ceased to exist.

Chapter Eighteen

She woke to a pounding head, reluctantly opening her eyes only to find she was blindfolded. Trying to move she found that her arms were chained so they were fully stretched out. Rolling her neck she tried to get the ache out of it from sleeping strung up. Her mouth felt dry, her arms and neck ached and she had a killer headache. Mentally checking her surroundings, she found no one in the room with her and couldn't search beyond it.

An image came to her of Ronan chained to a wall like this, when they'd been caught by Paili. She pushed it from her mind, refusing to give into the fear that tried to fill her. At least she wasn't bleeding to death like he'd been. She had other things to focus on instead of worrying about the past.

Where was she and what had happened to Kade? Did they get him too? And the other dragons that had been watching her, what had happened to them? "Let me out!" Screaming made her throat hurt. She needed a drink. And wanted to use the bathroom. Tugging on the chains didn't help. They were tight against her wrists, stretching her arms so she barely had any movement.

"Face me cowards!" Again she tugged on the chains. Nothing. She was stuck hanging on the wall. "I'm going to kill you when I get out of here!" And she would get out. Somehow. Anger overrode fear. "My dragons will hunt you down and tear your hearts from your bodies!" That's if she didn't do it first. How dare they chain her up like this. And where was Kade? She needed to know what had happened to him.

No one answered. The room remained empty. She couldn't smell anything to give her a clue to her surroundings. No sounds, no scents, nothing. Again she tugged at the chains. They were too tight for her to change form. She was stuck here. Swearing, she rattled the chains. Still no one answered. Her mouth was dry and her throat was scratchy, her headache no better.

No one was coming. They'd chained her up and left her here. She had no idea how much time passed before she heard the door being unlocked. All she knew was that it had to have been hours. The anger that had faded rushed back in as the door swung open with a soft creak.

She breathed deep, instantly recognising the scents. "You're wasting your time blindfolding me." No one answered. The only sound was footsteps. "Wayne. Stanley. Vikki. Jennifer. Dominic. I can smell each of you and you're all dead."

"You told me the smoke would make it impossible for her to smell us," Stanley said.

"It works on dragons," Wayne said.

Amber smiled, impersonating Ronan's most predatory one. "I'm not a dragon. I don't think like a dragon or even act like a dragon. But for all of you, I'll make an exception. If you let me go, I'll give you a head start. Keep me chained and when I get out of here, I'll tear your hearts out." She probably couldn't do it, but they wouldn't know that. She heard footsteps come closer and smelled Vikki near her.

Vikki pulled the blindfold from Amber's eyes, smiling. "You're not getting out of here. There's no one to come to your rescue."

"None of my dragons will stop looking for me until they find me."

"It's a little hard to hunt someone down when you're dead."

Amber froze, not even able to breathe. No! Her gaze held Vikki's trying to figure out if she told the truth. "You lie."

Vikki laughed. "He tried so hard to save you, throwing himself into the smoke. It took six bullets before his heart finally stopped beating. There were others. Only one escaped, but he was badly wounded."

Pain arrowed through her. Not Kade. They couldn't have killed Kade. One had survived. Maybe it had been Kade. She could have healed him. Who had survived? Ronan. It was always Ronan. He wouldn't have fought a losing battle. It was always him. Burning hot rage raced through her, numbing the pain. "You better hope I never escape." Her words were soft, an edge to them she'd never heard before.

Vikki laughed, turning away from her to cross the room. "Dominic, go and fetch me a chair. I need to have a little chat with our new pet."

Amber watched Dominic open the door, not quite closing it when he left. She tried to reach out, but it looked like it wasn't just this room guarded against dragon and mage abilities. Her gaze travelled the room. It was empty of all furniture and furnishings. Only the chains on the walls. A bare bulb was fitted to the ceiling and there wasn't even a window. The rest of the Knights watched her. What were they waiting for?

Dominic returned with a timber chair, placing it in the middle of the room. Vikki sat down, a smile still on her face. She crossed her legs, her gaze remaining on Amber.

"Whatever you want, you won't get it," Amber said.

"Oh, I think we will. You see, we have your daddy. Surely you don't want anything to happen to him."

Amber glared at Vikki. "I don't believe you."

"That's too bad. He's the one who'll suffer if you don't tell us what we want to know."

"Prove it. Bring him here."

"We can't do that right now. He's in a secure place. As soon as we can we'll bring him here. You know I was the one who came up with the idea to break up your parents. And it worked. Your mother went running back to your grandmother so we could find out where Helen was living. But your grandparents aren't the Knights they once were. It was a waste of time."

"You don't care about my father?"

Vikki laughed. "Of course not. He isn't a Knight and he's the most boring man imaginable. I certainly won't lose any sleep over his torture. Will you?"

Vikki rose to her feet. "We'll be back in a couple of hours, maybe then you'll be willing to tell us everything you know about dragons and where to find them."

She doubted it. There was no way she trusted any of them. No matter what deal they offered. "I want a drink of water."

Vikki laughed. "You're not getting anything until you tell us what we want to know."

"There's laws against prisoner mistreatment." She had no idea what they were called or exactly what they were, but these were humans, surely they'd know.

This time it was Stanley who laughed. "They only apply to humans and you're not human. Not even close."

She tugged at her chains again. "To think I actually felt sorry for you."

"I don't want your pity, dragon," Stanley spat.

Vikki strode to the door. "Time to go. Let's see how thirsty she is when we get back."

Amber watched them go, hearing the door lock behind them. She felt like screaming, but refused to give them that satisfaction. When she got out of here, they were dead. Every last one of them. She tried not to think of Kade, tried not to think of six bullets entering his body, but it was impossible. She'd heard a gun before whatever had been on that cloth had knocked her out. Had that been the first bullet? Or the last one? There'd been shots earlier.

She hung there, her rage growing and she finally understood Ronan's need to kill. The rage she'd felt at seeing a gun pointed at her mother's head was nothing compared to this. A sharp cutting pain pierced the anger and her hands curled into fists. They would pay in blood.

She remembered standing near Ronan's water garden and him asking her, 'Would you avenge me if someone killed me?'

And she'd thought it was a dragon emotion. No, it was human too. Ronan just wasn't the one to drive her to that emotion. Kade was. Closing her eyes she fought against the pain that made her want to cry out. He couldn't be dead. Vikki had to be lying. But she'd looked so satisfied when she'd spoken the words. So proud. Like she'd been the one to pull the trigger. All six times. She had to get out of here. Again she tugged at the chains. They held tight.

She fumed and raged internally, coming up with and discarding outlandish plans, the panther prowling restlessly within her. When Vikki returned, she only had Wayne with her. "What happened to the rest? Dragons get them already?"

"They had classes. It's business as usual at the headquarters. Your dragon that escaped hasn't attacked us. He thinks it was dragons that took you." Vikki sat on the timber chair.

Wayne smiled. "Probably had something to do with the dragon blood we spilled. Always good to take trophies from your kills. You never know when they'll come in handy."

"The Knights all headed out to the archery range just like they do every other Saturday afternoon. And no one even cares that you're missing."

It was nearly a full day since she'd been captured. No wonder she was hungry and thirsty. If she wasn't chained, Vikki wouldn't be smiling like that. "When I escape you better run because I'm going hunting and I won't stop until all of you are dead."

"You don't get it, do you?" Vikki asked. "You're never getting free. Ever."

"Then why would I bother telling you anything? Ever." She mockingly repeated Vikki's last word.

"To save your father."

"Where is he? I don't believe you've got him. Anyway, it doesn't matter. I'll be dead before you get anything out of me."

Wayne slowly crossed the room, his used car salesman smile firmly in place. "You're not the type to kill yourself. You're a fighter."

"I didn't say I'd kill myself. I said I'd be dead. When I become a panther these chains will rip me apart."

Vikki joined her brother. "Simple. Don't become a panther."

"It's not simple. If I don't eat and drink the panther will break free looking for her own meal." She watched as Vikki and Wayne shared a look.

Vikki looked her up and down. "I don't believe you."

Amber tried to shrug but it was impossible. "Doesn't change the facts just because you don't believe them." She growled, the panther smelling prey at the flash of fear that went through Wayne. Her eyes narrowed. "Who do you answer to?"

"I answer to no one," Vikki said.

Amber laughed, a sound that Ronan would have been proud of, nodding towards Wayne. "Then why was he afraid at the thought I might die? See how close the panther is? She can smell the fear in your sweat. Who do you answer to? Is it Martin? Is that why Dominic was here?"

Wayne glanced towards his sister. She pushed him away, getting in Amber's face. "We answer to no one. You will tell us where to find the dragons and then I'll feed you."

Amber laughed. "You're afraid. You're both afraid. What is it you fear?"

"I fear no one. No human, no dragon. But you will feel fear. When your father is brought before you and we start to torture him, then you'll feel fear." Vikki spun on her heel, striding for the door.

"I need to eat!"

Vikki didn't look back. "Wayne. Let's go."

Amber growled, trying to escape. "Another couple of hours and it could be too late."

Wayne glanced over his shoulder at Amber, twice, before he reached the door.

She heard Vikki's footsteps fade into the distance. "Do you understand, Wayne? I can't control her forever. When I turn I will be torn apart. It might save you from me hunting you down, but it won't save you from whoever you answer to."

Wayne watched her a moment longer before he closed the door, his smile no longer in place.

She screamed, the sound more like that of a panther roaring than anything human. Her hands curled into fists. They had to feed her. She wanted to kill them for taking Kade from her and she couldn't do that if she died.

Time passed slowly. She raged, tried to escape, yelled for food. No one answered her. No one came. She did everything but think of Kade. The pain and anger were too much for the panther to handle. Not if she wanted to keep her contained.

By the time she heard someone unlocking the door, she had to force herself not to beg them to let her go. She was starving, desperate to use the bathroom and her body ached from being chained for so long. The door swung open. "You!"

Jennifer laughed, dropping an esky onto the floor and pulling a gun from the back of her jeans. "I'm guessing that greeting isn't for me." She stepped into the room. "You know I don't think she likes you anymore, Roy."

Roy shrugged, pointing his gun at Amber. "Not my problem." Then directly to Amber. *"Play along. I'm trying to get you out of here."*

"I should have let you die." She glared at him. *"Do you really expect me to believe that when you've got a gun pointed at me?"*

"It's taken me all this time to convince Jennifer that I can be trusted. Lucky she's always had a crush on me." Roy grinned. "Your mistake."

"If you're here to help me then point that gun at Jennifer, not me." She growled. "If you don't let me out of here

I'm going to hunt you down too. I'll tear your heart out and turn it to ash."

"Dad's an idiot telling us to feed her. We should just let her starve. I'm sure we can find Gold Dragons without her help."

"Let's get it over with. You unlock one of her arms and I'll hold the gun on her," Roy said.

"Don't order me around, Roy. I could have brought Dominic. I didn't need to bring you."

Roy laughed. "Yeah, but I'm more fun to be with."

"He has his uses." Jennifer came closer, tucking the gun she carried in the back of her jeans. "Don't try anything or he will shoot."

"I need to use the bathroom."

"No one said anything about bathrooms. Only food." Jennifer unlocked one of Amber's hands, quickly stepping back.

Her arm dropped to her side and she couldn't hold back a gasp as feeling returned to it. "I need to use the bathroom before I can eat."

"Promise me you won't do anything stupid. I will come back for you. When I get rid of Jennifer." Roy remained by the door. "Why should we trust you not to try and escape?"

"Why not help me escape now? Shoot Jennifer and we can get out of here."

"Because we're not the only ones here. We'd be killed before we made it to the front door." Then out loud. "Come on, Amber. Tell me."

"Why should I trust you?"

"I owe you my life."

Amber stared at him a moment longer. *"I promise."* Then out loud. "Because I'm too weak to do anything." She spat the words out like they were the last ones she wanted to admit.

"Unlock her."

"Stop ordering me around. And are you stupid? She'll escape."

Roy shook his head. "I'll shoot her. Besides, if she gets past us she won't get past your father and Stanley."

Jennifer pointed her gun at Roy. "If she escapes, I'll shoot you."

"She won't escape. Now unlock the other chain."

Jennifer continued to hold the gun on Roy. Minutes passed before she tucked it into the back of her jeans. As soon as she'd unlocked the second chain, she backed up, drawing the gun again. "Move it, bitch."

Chapter Nineteen

Amber fought pain as feeling came back into her arms. It was a lot easier to fight the pain than the urge to change form and tear Jennifer's throat out.

"Amber." There was a warning in Roy's voice. *"You promised."*

Her gaze left Jennifer, travelling across the room to Roy, who was stepping out of the doorway. She stalked across the room, her mind searching for others. She could find none, but she also couldn't range far. "Where are they?"

"Who?" Jennifer demanded.

"Your father and Stanley. They're not nearby."

"There's another door. It's locked. They're upstairs." Roy gestured to his right. "Bathroom is that way."

"Have you told anyone I'm here?"

"I didn't know. Jennifer didn't tell me until we got here.

I kept saying how I wished I could congratulate whoever took you even if it was a dragon and stuff like that. Even that I could almost kiss them. After archery Jennifer said she wanted to show me something, but I had to promise not to tell anyone. A Knight's word is binding, Amber. We're honour bound to keep it."

She opened the door at the end of the corridor, finding a bathroom. *"So you're not going to help me?"*

"I will. I just can't tell anyone."

Amber closed the bathroom door, cutting off access to Roy's mind.

"Don't take too long in there," Jennifer warned.

She had a mouthful of water from the hand basin before she used the toilet, having a larger drink after she'd washed her hands. A search of the room showed it was the same as the room she was kept in. No windows and no way to contact the outside world. Roy better keep his word to help her. She opened the door.

Jennifer walked backwards. "All right, back to the room."

"When you're in the room, we'll put one chain on you and then you can have something to eat." Roy kept the gun trained on her and he also walked backwards.

"You don't have to keep that gun pointed at me. I won't break my promise."

"It'd make Jennifer suspicious if I didn't."

"Did you kiss her?"

Roy glanced away. *"I'll no longer owe you for saving my life once I get you out of here."*

Amber laughed. *"It couldn't have been that bad."*

"What are you laughing at?"

"I've been trying to avoid it for years."

Amber raised her left hand so Jennifer could put the chain on it. "I'm laughing at you. There's only one of me, but you're terrified."

Jennifer snapped the manacle around Amber's wrist. "I am not."

She breathed in deeply, closing her eyes as she did. A smiled curved her lips. "I can smell the fear. And you better be afraid. I'm going to hunt you down when I escape."

Jennifer took a step away, pointing the gun at Amber's face. "Shut up."

Roy tucked his gun into the back of his jeans. "Don't shoot her, Jennifer." He picked up the esky. "We're meant to be feeding her. Not killing her." He opened the esky and took out a lidded, plastic container.

Amber's mouth watered when he removed the lid

of the container, the panther trying to break free. Her hands curled into fists as she tried to hold her back. When Roy held out a fork, a piece of roast meat on it, she took it, barely managing to stop herself from tearing it off the fork. She speared another piece of roast meat from the container Roy held up. Jennifer paced the room, complaining about how long it was taking.

As soon as Amber had eaten the last piece, Jennifer came to a halt. "Finally. Now give me your other arm so I can chain you up."

Amber met Roy's gaze, trying to find any deception. *"You better come back for me."*

"I promise."

She raised her hand, gritting her teeth as the manacle snapped closed. *"If you don't, I will find my own way out and I will hunt you down."*

Roy followed Jennifer to the door. *"I promise I'll return."* The door shut, closing her out of his mind.

She tugged at the chains, wanting to scream at them to come back. How dare they chain her? Thoughts of Kade crept back into her mind. How dare they! The panther prowled in her and she tried to control her anger. Images filled her mind. Ones of blood. Oceans of blood. But this time it wasn't friends and family. This time it was the Knights who'd done this to her. Pulling on the chains, she growled. They'd pay. In blood.

She stared at the door, willing Roy to return. But it wasn't Roy who unlocked the door next. It was Stanley. He grinned as he strode towards her.

"Smile while you can. It won't be long before you'll never smile again."

He laughed. "You can't do anything while you're chained up like that. Those manacles are the same ones that stop dragons from changing. I tried to tell Wayne you wouldn't be able to change, but he didn't want to risk it. He won't always be here though. When he leaves you in my care next week there won't be any food until you talk."

"Mages are different to dragons. They won't stop me from changing."

"I guess we'll see."

Amber eyed him, smelling no fear on him. "You don't know, do you?"

"Know what?"

"Whoever's pulling their strings. They haven't told you. Why haven't they told you who they answer to? Don't they trust you?"

"There is no one else. Dragons always lie. You can't be trusted."

Amber smiled in answer.

"You're going to regret ever joining the dragons."

"You're the one who'll have regrets. But don't worry. You won't have them for long. I hear the dead have no regrets." She thought of Kade and the panther roared inside her, wanting to escape.

"Are you ready to talk?"

"Never." The word was a growl.

"Never is a long time when you're chained to a wall." Stanley stood, arms crossed. When she remained silent he eventually turned away and left, locking the door.

Where was Roy? How long did he expect her to wait? If he'd lied to her she would kill him slowly. Maybe give him to Ronan before he died and then see how much he enjoyed breaking promises.

When the door swung open again, it was Roy, holding her sword and daggers. "What took you so long?"

"They can hear. Be quiet," Roy thought to her.

"Then unlock me and let's get out of here."

Roy put her weapons on the seat in the centre of the room. *"We don't have much time now."* He unlocked the first manacle.

"What took you so long?"

"I had to get permission to take Jennifer to see a movie."

"Where is she?" When he unlocked the second

manacle, she rubbed at her wrists, heading for the chair.

"In the boot of my car."

Amber grinned. *"Sounds like a good place for her."* She strapped on her weapons. *"Do you know where my bracelets are?"*

"Upstairs. What do you need them for?"

There was no way she'd break a promise to Ronan and tell Roy the truth about her jewellery. *"Sentimental reasons."* She looked him up and down, thinking of his earlier comment about having to kiss Jennifer, grinning in relief at escaping. *"You know, I could almost kiss you."*

Roy took a step away. *"Please don't. I know how possessive dragons are of their property. If you're dating a dragon, he'll think he owns you."*

Amber's grin faded. Once she would have said, 'Nah, I own him.' Pain nearly overwhelmed her and she held herself still as she battled it. They would pay for taking Kade from her.

"Hurry up. They'll be on their way here. You shouldn't have spoken aloud."

"You should have warned me." She ran beside him along the corridor, headed for the closed door at the top of a set of stairs.

"You didn't give me a chance." Roy ran up the stairs, reaching for the door.

It burst open and Vikki stood there, gun in hand. "I knew we shouldn't have trusted you. What have you done to Jennifer?"

Roy backed down the stairs. "She's alive. Let us out and I'll tell you where she is." He drew his sword.

Vikki laughed. "Do you really think that's going to help you against a gun?"

"I guess we'll see." Roy continued to back down the stairs.

Amber wasn't about to wait and see. She leapt at Vikki, becoming a panther in mid leap. The gun went off as it was knocked from Vikki's hand. Vikki tumbled down the steps jumping to her feet as she hit the bottom, drawing her sword. When Roy would have attacked, Amber said to him, *"There's someone upstairs. I'll take care of Vikki. You check upstairs."*

Roy rushed past Amber, who turned human, as Vikki attacked her. Amber dodged the sword that came for her, drawing her own to block the next attack. She barely managed to block the flurry of attacks that ended up driving her down the corridor. There was no way she could beat Vikki in a sword fight. Dropping her sword she launched herself into the air, becoming a goshawk, landing behind Vikki to turn human. Drawing her daggers, Amber attacked Vikki who dodged the worst of the strike.

"Stanley told me all about your little tricks. There's nothing you can do that I won't expect."

"He's really only seen me fight once." She watched as Vikki remained still, her sword at the ready.

"It doesn't matter. Once he's taken care of Roy he'll be down here to help me deal with you. If you last that long."

She thought of Kade. "You'll be the one who won't last long." In one move she sheathed her daggers and became a panther. Vikki's sword sliced across her skin, the scent of blood filling the corridor as Vikki's sword was jarred from her hand, spinning across the floor. The force of the attack slammed Vikki against the floor. Amber barely managed not to tear her throat out. She turned human continuing to pin Vikki down. "I told you I'd come hunting you once I was free."

"You can't win. Stanley will be here soon. Roy doesn't stand a chance against him."

"Why? Are you going to kill him like you killed Kade?"

"He's a traitor. He deserves to die like all dragons do."

Anger and pain rushed through her. "I'm going to

cut out your heart." Amber smelt the fear before she saw it in Vikki's eyes.

"No. He's alive. I lied."

The fear she could smell on Vikki made the panther stir. "I don't believe you."

Vikki struggled to escape. "He is. I lied. Let me go. Please."

Fighting to keep Vikki pinned she pulled a dagger from its sheath, drawing it back. "I told you I'd kill you. How many bullets did you say it was again?"

"I lied. There was none. Or maybe only one. Please. He's still alive. Wounded but alive. Don't kill me."

"Liar."

"No! You don't know what's coming. We need a live Gold Dragon. We have to stop them. Please. Don't kill me."

"You're lucky I'm in a hurry." She plunged the dagger into Vikki's heart, blood gushing out as she withdrew the dagger.

There was a look of surprise on Vikki's face as hands clutched her chest. "The hounds. The hounds are coming." Her eyes closed and Amber could no longer hear the beat of her heart.

She rose to her feet and stared down at Vikki, the blood spreading across the floor. Hounds or Hound?

The only Hound she knew was Ronan's son. Surely he wouldn't go against his father. That'd be suicidal. Stepping back before the pool of blood reached her feet, she swore as she realised what she'd done. She'd just killed her father's girlfriend. Even though she wasn't much of one, her father hadn't known that. There was no way she was going to be the one to tell him. Besides, Vikki shouldn't have killed her boyfriend. Pain sliced through her as she thought of Kade and she wanted to kill Vikki again. Her hand curled into a fist as she fought against letting the panther escape.

With the dagger still in her hand she collected her sword, sheathing it as she headed for the stairs. She wasn't even halfway up when a shot rang out on the floor above. Sheathing the dagger, she took the rest of the steps two at a time, bursting into a kitchen.

Stanley looked up, the gun still aimed at Roy who was sprawled on the floor. He backed away, raising the gun to point it at Amber. "What have you done? Where's Vikki."

"Dead." She mentally reached for Roy. He was alive but unconscious. "Like you will be."

"Don't come any closer."

Amber continued to move forward. "Or what?"

Stanley aimed the gun at Roy. "Or I'll shoot him."

Not trusting Stanley, Amber raced forward, the gun going off before she had a chance to tackle him. When she collided with him the gun skittered across the kitchen floor. She was on her feet almost instantly, rushing to Roy's side, her hand pressing against the wound in his chest. As she tried to heal him she heard Stanley rise to his feet, running from the kitchen. Keeping a hand pressed against Roy's wound she fought the urge to chase after Stanley. Roy wouldn't survive if she didn't heal him. If Roy died, his family would be out for her blood. She had more than enough wanting her dead. She remembered his expression when he'd told her she'd saved him. Wary, uncertain, a touch of fear. And his worry that he was a traitor if they were allies. She wasn't about to let him die. Rage burned through her that she hadn't been there to do this for Kade. That Vikki, Wayne and Stanley had stolen the opportunity from her.

The flow of blood slowed as the wound closed, eventually stopping. But still Roy remained unconscious. Exhausted, Amber stumbled to her feet, her gaze scanning the kitchen. On the table were her bracelets and phone. Striding across the kitchen she grabbed her bracelets and slipped them on, drawing power from one of them. As she picked up her phone and turned it on she mentally reached for Ronan. Her knees nearly gave way when she found Kade not far from him. Her phone dropped to the table as she clutched the edge of it.

He was alive? But Vikki had looked so satisfied and proud when she'd told her. And she'd heard gunshots. Her fingers tightened on the table edge. Pain, anger and relief rushed through her, making her feel light headed. Her phone finished turning on and beeped its missed messages. Ignoring the messages, Amber dialled Kade's number. Her hands were shaking so hard it was an effort to make the call.

Chapter Twenty

Kade answered on the first ring. "Amber! Where are you?"

"You're okay?"

"Forget about me. Where are you?"

"They told me you were dead."

"I'm alive. Where are you, Amber?" He spoke slower, softer, like he was addressing a crazy person.

Maybe she was crazy. Her legs wanted to give out, but she didn't let them, clinging to the edge of the table as she again looked around. "I don't know." She momentarily closed her eyes when she heard the panic in her voice. She couldn't go to pieces yet, Stanley might return with help.

"Who was it? Tell me Amber, who was it?"

Before Amber could answer, Roy groaned. She crossed the room on unsteady legs, crouching beside him to help him sit up.

"Amber? Who's there with you?"

"Roy."

"Was he one of the ones who took you?"

"No."

"Then what's going on? Where are you? Tell me where you are." The calm disappeared from his voice leaving demands and fear.

"How the hell would I know?" She shouted the words into the phone, trying desperately to hold things together. She'd killed someone. Plunged a knife into her heart. At the end Vikki had told her the truth. Kade was alive. If she hadn't lied to her… her thoughts trailed off. She didn't know. She just didn't know what she would have done.

"What happened?" Roy stared around the kitchen. "Where's Stanley? And Vikki?"

"Stanley got away. We have to get out of here." Amber helped him to his feet, avoiding the second question.

"Amber?" Kade's voice softened, but there was still worry in it.

Roy staggered and she wrapped an arm around his waist. Kade was alive. But she still ached, thinking that he might have died. "She said you were dead." They walked towards the door, gathering Roy's sword as they passed it.

"Who did?"

"Vikki."

"I'll kill her."

The fierceness in his voice echoed the way she'd felt when she'd thought him dead. She stepped out into the night, still supporting Roy. "You're too late." The words were a whisper.

There was silence before Kade spoke. "You okay, Amber?"

"I don't know."

"Are you hurt?"

"That way." Roy sheathed his sword before he pointed out the direction.

"Amber?"

She didn't know how to answer Kade. "Where's Ronan?"

"He's waiting for me to find out where you are." There was another pause. "He won't wait much longer. What can you see, Amber?"

"It's dark. What do you think I can see?" She alternated between annoyance and relief. "I don't have a clue where I am." There was a touch of panic in her voice and she took a deep breath. It was a bad idea. The smell of blood made the panther want to escape.

"Amber." Ronan spoke on the phone.

A fierce protectiveness rushed over her. She couldn't go through that again. Couldn't listen to someone tell her Kade was hurt. That he was dead. "What did you do to Kade?"

"Nothing, kitten. He's pacing the floor again. Where are you?"

Roy tried to pull away from her, pointing to a sedan parked on the side of the road. "My mum's car." He fumbled for his car keys, dropping them when he finally fished them out of his pocket.

Amber leaned him against the car while she picked them up, unlocking the car and helping Roy onto the seat.

"Amber?"

She started to answer, but a banging in the boot drew her attention. She looked down at Roy when he grabbed her arm.

"Let her out. Please."

Amber shook him off her. "She wanted to kill me."

"Let her go. She's my prisoner. Just let her go."

"Amber!"

She ignored Ronan, staring at Roy a moment longer. "She'll want revenge."

Roy shrugged. "Let her out. She's only in there because I tricked her."

"Answer me, Amber."

She strode towards the boot, the key still in her hand. "Where are you, Ronan?"

"At my house. What's going on? And who wants revenge?"

"Jennifer. I'm setting her free."

"Are you crazy?"

The phone nearly vibrated with his anger. Amber smiled slightly. "Probably." She thought about it for another second. "More than likely." Opening the boot, she stared down at Jennifer in the dim light from the boot. She was gagged and tied and there was enough light to see the anger in her eyes. There was no doubt she wanted revenge. "I'll call you back in a minute, Ronan." She hung up on his protests, sliding the phone into her pocket. It started ringing almost instantly.

Ignoring the phone, Amber heaved Jennifer out, dumping her on the footpath. "The house is that way." She pointed in the direction as Jennifer struggled to her feet, slamming the boot shut. Leaving Jennifer tied and gagged Amber strode around to the driver's seat, her phone still ringing.

"We have to get out of here before Stanley brings Wayne back."

Amber nodded, starting the car. The moment her phone stopped ringing it rang again. She swore. Did

Ronan ever give up? She smiled wryly. What was she thinking? Of course he didn't.

"You going to answer that?"

Amber ignored both the phone and Roy as she drove down the street. Searching out Ronan's direction, she turned the next corner. She had no idea where she was, but she knew how to track Ronan and Kade. When she was headed in the right direction Amber answered her phone noticing Ronan was ringing from his own phone this time.

"I'm heading your way."

"Who was it, Amber? Who took you? We found dragon blood once the smoke had cleared, but Knights are the ones who use the smoke to hide their scent. Not dragons."

"Wayne and Vikki. And Stanley, but I don't think he knew exactly what was going on."

"What was going on, kitten?"

"I don't know, but I think there's someone else. Vikki mentioned Hound."

"Are you sure? What exactly did she say?"

Amber tried to remember, but what was clearest was all the blood. "I think she said the hounds are coming."

"Is that it?"

"Yes."

"Well why didn't you ask her what she meant?"

"I didn't get the chance. I'd already stabbed her in the heart by then."

Ronan chuckled.

"It's not funny!" Amber shouted at Ronan.

"No, what isn't funny is that they thought they could kidnap you and there'd be no consequences." There was a moment's silence before Ronan spoke again. "Is Wayne still alive?"

"Wasn't killing Vikki enough for you?" Amber ignored the noise Roy made beside her. She couldn't help thinking about Vikki's threat. "Is my dad safe?"

"Yes. I still have a Gold watching him. How did you get away?"

"Roy."

"Why?"

"Does this matter right now?"

"It always matters, kitten."

"Yeah well, all I'm worried about at the moment is getting as far away from that place as possible."

"Where are you? We'll come and get you."

Anger flared again. "Will everyone stop asking me that? I wouldn't have a-" She stopped abruptly as she spotted a landmark she recognised. "Actually. I might know where I am. Or where I'll be in a minute." She gave him the location she was now headed for. She barely managed to pull up before Kade was opening the driver's door and crushing her to him. She clung to him, burying her face against his chest, breathing in the scent of him. Listening to the beat of his heart.

"I'm going to kill them," Kade said against her hair.

Amber couldn't help thinking of the gun Stanley carried and the sound of gunshots when she'd been kidnapped. There was no way she was letting Kade out of her sight. "Not without me you're not."

Kade pulled back enough to meet her gaze. "You want to go kill someone?"

Amber ignored the disbelief she could see in his eyes and hear in his tone. She jabbed at his chest with a finger. "Not on your own." When his breath caught she tugged at his shirt. "What's wrong?"

He tried to push her hands away. "I'm okay."

She finally managed to get his shirt up high enough to see his chest and side. His skin was sewn together in two places, the stitches reminding her of the first night she'd met him. "They shot you?"

Ronan dragged Kade away from the car door. "Come on, kitten. You can heal him later. We need to get back to my place."

Amber got out of the car, pushing Ronan out of the way with the flat of her hand against his chest. She was not in the mood to put up with Ronan's orders.

"I don't care where you're going, but I'm going back to Kade's place, having a shower and going to bed. And if you're lucky I'll find the time to see you in the morning."

When Amber started to walk past him, Ronan grabbed her upper arm. "It's not secure enough."

She met his gaze, searching the depths of his blue eyes with the help of the streetlight. "Is anywhere?"

Ronan stared at her for a moment before nodding towards Roy who had come to stand near her. "What am I meant to do with him?"

"Do we have our Gold here?" Amber asked Kade directly. When he nodded, and called the Gold out of the Void, she said to Ronan, "He'll come with us." She pulled away. "Make sure the car gets returned to the Knights' headquarters."

Ronan stepped in front of her, blocking her escape. "Don't you dare get yourself killed, kitten."

"Yeah, I know. You still have a use for me." Her voice was filled with bitterness. She stepped around him, reaching for Kade. *"Get us out of here."*

Kade took them through the Void to arrive on his front verandah. A Gold deposited Roy beside them before immediately disappearing back into the Void. Kade turned to Roy. "You can stay in Orin and Morgan's room."

"I have to warn my family."

For a moment Amber felt annoyed with Ronan for making her wonder about Roy's motives. It didn't take her long to admit to herself that she would have been wondering about them anyway. "Why did you come after me?"

"Ronan told my uncles that if anything happened to you while I was guarding you he'd hold them personally responsible. That they'd wish for death if I didn't protect you."

Amber started to reassure him when she saw the worry in his eyes, but stopped. Ronan never made threats, only promises. She finally came up with something she could say instead. "He won't hurt them over this. Not after all you've done to help me."

Maira opened the front door, Brann on her heels. She beckoned to Roy. "I'll show you to your room and get you a change of clothes so you can wash before you go to bed. I'm sure you don't want to sleep with all that blood on you."

Amber watched as Roy followed Maira and Brann, leaving the door open behind him. After tonight, his family could take care of him. She had more than enough people to look out for. When her phone rang and she saw it was her grandmother she groaned, closing her eyes as she leaned against Kade. Speaking to one of her grandparents was the last thing she wanted to do right now.

Kade looked at the screen of her phone. "They were really worried when you were taken Friday afternoon."

"I'm not going back there." She continued to hold the phone, staring at it until it stopped ringing.

"You don't have to worry about that. It was Knights that kidnapped you. Ronan's been trying to get you out of the deal since they didn't protect you. Knowing that it was some of their people who kidnapped you should make it easier."

"Well he's going to have to make sure he does get me out of the deal because I'm not going back. Ever." She couldn't help thinking of Vikki saying the word ever to her. She shied from that thought, taking a step away from Kade and linking her fingers through his to tug him towards the doorway. "Come inside so I can deal with your wounds." Her phone started ringing again and when she saw it was her grandmother she growled.

"It might be best to answer. I don't think they're going to give up."

With another growl, Amber answered the phone. "What?"

"Why didn't you ring us? Why did we have to hear from Ronan that you had escaped?"

She was so not in the mood for this. Stepping into the lounge room she headed for one of the armchairs and was about to sit down when she remembered the blood. Not sure that it would all be dry she remained standing. "I plan to have a shower, something to eat and then go to bed." She didn't bother mentioning Kade's wounds she needed to heal because she doubted her grandmother would care.

"So your family are less important to you then the dragons. You couldn't even be bothered giving us a chance."

"How much of a chance did the Knights give me? Kidnapping me, chaining me to a wall and threatening to torture my father is not what I'd call giving someone a chance."

"They will be dealt with."

"How?"

"Martin will reprimand them for what they did."

"Reprimand!" Amber started to pace the lounge room floor. "Reprimand? It sounds like you're talking about a prank. Kidnapping is not a prank. Chaining someone up. Starving them. Threatening them. Those are not pranks." Anger flowed through her, making her pace the floor quicker, the panther stirring inside her. "If that's all they're going to get for what they did, then I'm glad I killed Vikki."

"You did what?"

"It was in battle. She was trying to stop me from escaping. Stanley tried to kill Roy."

"Was Roy injured?"

Amber stopped in mid pace remembering that Roy was meant to be a Knight, not a dragon. "I had to use my blood to heal him."

"You can heal Knights?"

"Sometimes." Maybe. "It's difficult." She had no real idea if she could do it. "But that's not the point. They tried to kill us. And what are you going to do about it? Oh that's right, tell them they were naughty and send them to bed without their dinner."

"I'd have thought that by now you'd be over your tendency to dramatise everything."

For a moment Amber was speechless. "You did not just say that. Dramatise? After the weekend I've had, I think I have the right to be more than a little upset." She started to pace again stepping around Kade who reached for her. "I'm going to bed. Don't bother ringing again tonight." She disconnected the call before her grandmother had a chance to say anything else. Heading for the bathroom, she hoped that Roy had already finished in there. She had just stepped out of the kitchen when a thought occurred to her and she stopped, spinning to face Kade who'd followed her. "Does Mum know?"

Kade shook his head. "I didn't think you'd want me to tell her."

"Thank you." She turned back in the direction of the bathroom, glad she didn't have to face her mother's hysterics. She had more than enough to deal with.

Chapter Twenty-One

It was Wednesday night and Amber stood at the foot of the bed, staring at it. She wasn't sure if there was even any point in trying to go to sleep. The last decent sleep she'd been able to have had been early Sunday morning when she'd dropped exhausted into bed, after her shower. She'd been putting it off, but knew it was well past time to ring Ronan. Taking out her phone, she didn't even get a chance to ring him before he was stepping out of the Void.

"I was about to ring you." She nodded towards her phone.

"You should have rung me Sunday night. Why didn't you?"

Amber shrugged.

"Why are you still going to school? No one has any idea where Wayne and Jennifer are. And they know where you live and where you go to school. You need to take better care of yourself than this."

"How could I forget? You need me to help you kill just one more person. Haven't I killed enough?" Her voice rose, but she couldn't stop it. She was tired, fed up with the nightmares she couldn't seem to stop and sick of worrying about every single person in her life and if they might be used as a hostage against her. She couldn't help thinking about Vikki's lies, that she'd held her father hostage. Next time someone said that it might even be the truth. Again. She pushed away the image of a gun held at her mother's head.

Kade opened the door, stepping into the room. "Why are you here, Ronan?"

He gestured towards Amber. "To see that she gets some sleep. Now that she no longer has to return to the Knights we can get on with the rest of our plans."

"Our plans?" Amber shook her head. "Don't you mean your plans?"

"No. Our plans. Aren't you my ally?"

She started to argue, barely managing to bite back her reply. "I'm really not in the mood for this, Ronan."

"We'll talk about it tomorrow. After you've slept." Ronan strode towards the bed, sitting on it to lean his back against the bed head, his legs stretched out in front of him. "Come on then." He gestured towards the space beside him.

Amber looked towards Kade. She'd really hoped that she would have been able to get past this without having to call Ronan. It somehow seemed worse that he'd turned up without her having to call him. She reached for Kade's mind, speaking directly to him. *"I was about to ring him when he turned up."*

Kade crossed the space that separated them pulling her tight against him. *"Get some sleep."*

"Okay." She held onto him for several minutes before she kissed him, stepping away slowly. *"I'll see you in the morning."* She held his gaze a moment longer before she turned and crossed the room, lying on the bed.

"You need more warriors to guard you."

Amber rolled onto her side, her back to Ronan. "I've got more than enough." She'd also turned down Amos' offer to protect her while they waited for Wayne to be found. He didn't like the fact they owed her for saving Roy's life, even if the reason he'd nearly died was because he'd been trying to rescue her.

"Go to sleep, kitten. We'll discuss it in the morning."

She was tempted to argue it now, but was too tired. Closing her eyes, her mind was filled with images of blood. They were instantly replaced by the coastline near Ronan's home, a rugged coastline with a sheer drop to jagged rocks in the ocean below. "Don't you know anywhere else to take me?" She turned towards Ronan. She saw that it was the real Ronan, not the image he presented to the rest of the world.

"Are you going to complain all night? I thought you wanted to get some sleep."

Amber smiled when she saw that once again he'd provided her with the same hand carved wooden bed as last time. "Where did you get this?"

Ronan growled. "If you don't hurry up and get in it I'll leave you to your nightmares." He sat on the edge of the cliff, letting his legs dangle over.

"I doubt it. That wouldn't help you at all."

Ronan held her gaze. "Go to sleep, kitten." He was silent a moment. "There will be no dreams tonight."

She continued to stare at him. In his real form he looked far too young to have done half the things she knew he'd accomplished. Far too young to have plotted and planned and become one of the most feared dragons. But he was, even if sometimes she forgot. Turning away she climbed into the bed snuggling down amongst the blankets. "When will it be?"

"When will what be?"

"When are we going after Tahmid?"

"Soon."

Frustration arrowed through her. Why couldn't Ronan answer a simple question? There was no one to hear what they said here. She partially sat up, resting back against her elbows and forearms as she looked over the mound of blankets. "How soon?"

"We'll talk about it tomorrow."

Amber growled dropping against the pillows. "Bloody annoying dragon," she muttered.

"Bloody annoying mage."

She held back a smile at the humour she heard in his voice. "Goodnight, Ronan." She closed her eyes, falling almost straight to sleep. When she woke in the morning she couldn't recall having had a single dream. Rolling over, she saw that Ronan still sat on the bed beside her. He stared down at her, once again his real form hidden.

"How do you feel?"

"I'm not sure I should answer that. You do know I have school today. You better not have planned anything."

"No plans for the day. But not long now."

Amber groaned, wanting to roll back over and pull the sheet over her head. Before she could say anything the bedroom door opened and Kade stepped inside.

"You look a lot better."

"Gee Kade, are you trying to tell me that lately I've been looking like crap?" Throwing back the sheet, she got out of bed, striding towards the open door.

Kade grinned. "I'd have to be an idiot to answer that question." He looked past Amber to Ronan who'd also risen from the bed. "I've talked with Flinn. We're going to turn the next fight into a test. Revenge for a kidnapping."

Ronan stared at Kade for a moment, speaking only to the two of them. *"You better make sure they think you're talking about the Knights."*

Kade nodded. *"We'll request permission to notify them at the last minute. It will cost gold to have them standing by waiting, but it's the safest way."*

"It will also help throw him off the scent. He'll think we're busy dealing with this latest problem. Make sure you mention the Knights during the conversation, but also have them word the test that it is revenge for a kidnapping, not revenge against the Knights."

"I'm not an idiot."

"I hope not because Tahmid still has access to all the details of the tests."

With a nod, Kade turned to Amber. "Breakfast is ready if you're hungry."

"Yeah."

When she started to follow Kade from the room, Ronan called out, "Kade."

Kade turned back to Ronan.

"Don't notify them until tomorrow. I have things to do first."

With another nod, Kade strode towards the kitchen. Amber followed him.

Chapter Twenty-Two

Her phone vibrated. While keeping an eye on the teacher, Amber withdrew it from her pocket. A glance showed it was Roy. *I need to talk to you. Face to face.* Returning her phone to her pocket she tried not to sigh. She hadn't seen or spoken to him since he'd left Sunday morning, having asked for her phone number first. She'd assured him that for now his secret was still safe. What else could he want to talk about? As soon as the bell rang to signal the end of that class Amber hurried to a secluded spot, telling Kade to join her. She showed him her message.

"When?"

She shrugged. "Now?"

"Where is he?"

Again she shrugged. "I'll find out." She dialled Roy's number and listened to it ring out. About to tell Kade that she couldn't get hold of him, her phone rang. It was Roy. "What's wrong?"

"I need to see you."

"Where are you?"

"At home. My mum will barely let me out of her sight. I don't know what she thought was going to happen when she let me train to be a Knight. Of course I'm going to get injured. Every Knight does at some stage."

Kade held out his hand. "Let me talk to him. I'll figure out somewhere we can meet him."

"Hang on, Roy." Amber held out the phone. "We need to be back before lunch is over. And back with enough time for me to have something to eat."

Taking the phone, Kade nodded.

She turned from him, stepping away from the edge of the building they hid beside. Her gaze was drawn to a group of girls laughing. That had once been her, Crystal and Angela. An eternity ago. Earlier this year. She wanted those days back. Wanted to know that the most dangerous thing she faced was breaking a fingernail. Now there was danger all around her and most of it she couldn't see until it was nearly too late.

Kade held out her phone to her. "You ready to go?"

Taking her phone and returning it to her pocket, she nodded.

Kade tugged her back against the side of the building before he took her through the Void to a park. Large leafy trees hid their exit from the Void.

"Where are we?"

"As close as I can get to where we'll meet Roy." Kade strode towards the road, where a taxi was waiting for them.

"How did you organise this?" She hopped in the back seat, Kade sliding in beside her.

"I didn't. Maira did." He grinned before he turned to the driver, giving him their destination.

Ten minutes later, they pulled up at another park. Roy stood on the concrete footpath waiting for them. Amber followed him deeper into the park, Kade at her side. When they stopped in the shadows under a large fig tree, Amber scanned the area. She couldn't help thinking about the fig tree out the front of the Knight's headquarters. The area was clear. No one else seemed to be in the park.

"What did you want to talk about?"

Roy shook his head glancing around. *"Not out loud."* When Amber nodded he continued. *"Ronan came to see me."*

"What did he want?"

"He wants me to set up a meeting with Tahmid. But it

has to be done today. He said this is what he wants me to do for him so he'll keep my secret for the year."

Amber could see straight away that Ronan had left himself a couple of loopholes. The year could be referring to this one that had nearly ended. And if he only offered to keep Roy's secret that didn't mean he'd keep Isaac, Amos and Eliza's secret. She was torn. Ronan was her ally, but Roy had come to her rescue. She didn't know what to do or say.

"Don't you think I should be helping him?"

Amber shook her head. *"I think you should help him, but you shouldn't be the one doing the negotiating."*

"Amber." Kade spoke directly to her, turning her name into a warning.

"Isn't he meant to be your ally?"

Amber nodded her gaze remaining on Roy when all she really wanted to do was keep checking their surroundings. *"Why did you want to talk to me about it?"*

Roy shrugged. *"I didn't have anyone else to talk to."* He shrugged again. *"I've heard a lot of stories about Ronan. None of them good. Are you sure he's your ally?"*

Amber laughed, a humourless sound that was becoming quite familiar to her lately. *"Yeah, but that's about all I'm sure of."*

"*Why would you basically tell me not to trust your ally?*"

She sobered, holding his gaze a moment before she spoke. "*Haven't you learned yet that you shouldn't trust anyone?*"

"*Does that mean I shouldn't trust you either?*"

"*Be careful, Amber. If you wreck things for Ronan he won't be happy with you.*" Kade spoke directly to her again.

She didn't even glance towards Kade, continuing to hold Roy's gaze. "*What did I just tell you?*"

Roy grinned. "*Maybe I'm a slow learner. You might have to repeat it.*"

Amber momentarily returned his grin. "*Do what Ronan wants, but don't go to him alone. Take your family with you.*"

Roy's grin faded. "*Why did you save me? Twice.*"

Why did he have to keep asking her this? "*Are you my enemy?*"

"*No.*"

"*Then why would I need to let you die?*"

"If you don't want to be late back to school we need to leave now," Kade said. Then directly to Amber, "*And it might be worth visiting Ronan and letting him know that you've been interfering again.*"

Amber laughed, unable to help herself. She spoke to Kade, *"You'd think he'd be used to it by now."* Then aloud to Roy, "Be careful."

Roy nodded.

Amber held out her hand to Kade, who took her through the Void to Ronan's water garden. A mental search of the area showed her that he wasn't there, but her phone rang after a couple of minutes. She smiled when she saw it was Ronan, guessing that someone had let him know they'd arrived. "Yeah."

"What are you doing?"

"I dropped in to visit you."

"Can it wait?"

"Would I have called in if it could? I don't have long, Ronan. I have to get back to school."

Ronan stepped out of the Void, disconnecting the phone call. "Did you tell the Golds where you were going so they could follow you?"

Amber glanced towards Kade.

"Our Gold was informed."

"But you didn't bother telling mine," Ronan said.

"I'm running out of time, Ronan."

He turned his gaze from Kade to Amber. "Why are you here?"

"Don't mess with Roy."

"Are you claiming him, kitten?"

She shook her head. "I just don't want any more problems. He'll help, but his family will negotiate for him. Haven't we got enough enemies amongst the Knights?"

"Just because they haven't killed you yet doesn't make them friends," Ronan warned.

"I know that. Haven't you told me enough times to trust no one?" She really hoped that Roy listened to that advice, especially when dealing with Ronan.

"Is that all? I have things to do."

"Yeah, I know. You're busy planning how to take over the world."

Ronan flashed her a grin. One of his highly predatory ones. "You're the one who seems to keep bringing that plan up. Are you sure you don't secretly wish to rule the world yourself, kitten?"

"Positive." She turned to Kade holding her hand out to him. "We need to go. We're probably already late."

Kade took her hand, taking her through the Void and back to school at the point where they'd left it. The school grounds were quiet. "I checked with Maira. She said class went in about five minutes ago."

Amber nodded, hurrying towards her classroom. So much for having time to eat. Hopefully she could keep the panther from escaping. Before she reached her class, her phone vibrated, letting her know a message had arrived. It was from Ronan. She smiled when she read it, certain one of his Golds would report her reaction to him. *You better not have messed up any of my plans.* Returning her phone to her pocket, she entered the classroom, a muttered sorry to the teacher as she made her way to her desk.

Chapter Twenty-Three

Friday night, Amber got a text from Crystal telling her to stand on Kade's verandah. Confused and curious, she told Kade before she headed outside. Kade stood beside her and she sent Crystal a text to let her know she was on the verandah. Crystal came out of the Void with Flinn.

Laughing, Amber rushed forward throwing her arms around her friend. Crystal was grinning and a quick look towards Flinn showed that he seemed extremely unimpressed. "When did Flinn learn how to use the void?"

"This morning. You can't believe how hard it was not to message you, but I wanted to surprise you. It's been the longest day ever."

Linking arms, Amber walked back towards the house with Crystal. "I can imagine."

Crystal's smile faded. "How are you? I wanted to

come and see you, but mum wouldn't let me. Talking on the phone and sending messages just isn't the same."

"I wanted to come and see you, but I had no idea how to explain a visit to your mum. Especially with how long it takes to drive there and back. Some things are much easier now my mum knows. Although she does tend to freak out a lot about it all." She dropped onto the couch tugging Crystal down with her. "How long can you stay?"

Crystal shrugged. "I have no idea. Flinn wants to learn some pathways. He didn't want to leave me alone. Well, with only his warriors to look after me. He wanted me to go to Temolae Keep. Said it was safest. As if you'd let anything happen to me."

They talked for several hours until Flinn returned to collect Crystal. He arrived on the verandah, opening the front door to tell Crystal 'hurry up' before he strode outside.

At the front door, Crystal threw her arms around Amber. "I can't wait until I move out of home and can visit you whenever I want."

"Move out of home?"

Crystal nodded. "Yep. As soon as school is over. I mean, who'd want to live with their parents when they can live in a castle?"

"Flinn is okay with you staying at the castle without him?"

"I'll be staying with him in Brisbane until the end of the year, but then we're going to the castle."

"Crystal–"

"It's okay. I know what you're going to say. There's nothing between us. Not like there is between you and Kade. I'll be fine. He's not about to let anything happen to me." Crystal grinned. "I'm more valuable than gold."

Amber laughed, hugging her friend again. "Of course you are." She reluctantly let her go. "Be careful."

"I will." Still grinning, Crystal crossed the space between her and Flinn, linking her arm through his. She barely had time to wave before they disappeared into the Void.

Amber continued to stand there, staring at the spot where Crystal had been.

Kade joined her at the front door, sliding his arm around her waist. "You coming inside or are you planning to stand here all night?"

She rested her head against his shoulder. "There never seems to be time for anything other than trying to survive."

Kade tugged her away from the door, closing it.

"Things will get better. They'll start to learn not to mess with us." He stared at her a moment. *"But you're going to have to start being a little more wary of Ronan. I think you're getting too close to him."*

Her eyes narrowed and she pulled away from Kade. *"What do you mean?"*

"You're beginning to think he's a friend. He's not. An ally is different from a friend. Don't trust him too much, Amber."

"I don't." Was she getting too close? No, surely not. She knew he wasn't a friend. But she wasn't clear about what exactly he was. Not like she'd once been. He mightn't be a friend, but he also wasn't a foe.

"Be careful." He reached for her, drawing her close. *"I don't want anything to happen to you."*

"Nothing will." She held onto him tightly. She didn't want anything to happen to Kade either. She recalled the pain she'd felt when Vikki had said Kade was dead. Her arms tightened as she closed her eyes, breathing in the scent of him, hearing the beat of his heart. She wasn't about to let anything happen to either of them.

Kade drew away from her. "Come on. Bed. You look tired." He walked with her to his bedroom door, leaving her there alone. Like the previous night,

Ronan stepped out of the Void as soon as Amber was in bed.

"I was beginning to think you were going to sit up giggling all night."

"You sound like you're upset we didn't invite you."

Ronan sat on the bed, leaning against the bed head. "Not likely. I would've been tempted to gag you for some peace if I'd been here."

She grinned. "Sure, Ronan. You probably would have joined in."

"Go to sleep, kitten."

Her grin faded. Was Kade right? Was she getting too friendly with Ronan? Once she'd been too terrified to joke so easily with him. Once she'd constantly been on her guard. Now, she didn't know what to think. But she did know that whatever plan Ronan was working on, it would be dangerous. Everything he'd done so far was dangerous. And she was certain he wanted to involve her in it, whatever it was.

"What's wrong, kitten?"

"It's getting closer, isn't it?"

He didn't even pretend not to understand. He nodded.

"It's probably going to scare the hell out of me and give me even more nightmares."

"*Interesting choice of words.*"

"*Is it? I wouldn't have a clue since you won't tell me anything.*"

Ronan chuckled. "Trust me, it's better that way. Now go to sleep."

She stared at him a moment longer before she closed her eyes. Like the last two nights, Ronan took her to the coastline of his home. Tonight she didn't speak as she snuggled into the blankets heaped onto the bed. Dread pooled in her at the thought of what was to come. She had a feeling it was going to be far worse than taking on Tahmid. Surely there was no way he could make her fall in with his plans. After Tahmid they would be even.

Her sleep was dreamless, but she woke with the same feeling of dread that she'd gone to sleep with. Before Ronan left the room, he stood beside the bed staring down at her. *"Be ready. We'll meet at your castle after lunch. Tell only Kade. I'll inform everyone else who needs to know."*

He disappeared into the Void before Amber could ask any questions. Growling, she threw her pillow. It sailed through the air, passing the place where Ronan had stood before it collided with the wall. It didn't make her feel any better.

Kade entered the room. "Are you okay?"

"No," she growled. Why couldn't Ronan have told her exactly what he was planning? Why all the secrecy? How hard was it to tell her in her mind what to expect instead of leaving her to wonder and worry. *"We need to meet Ronan at our castle after lunch. We're to tell no one."*

"We should have guessed that he'd plan something for either today or tomorrow. Especially since you keep telling him you need to finish school."

She flung back the sheets, rising to her feet. There was only two weeks left of school. "He better not think he can arrange all my days once school's out."

As soon as breakfast was eaten, Amber, Kade, Maira and Brann went to Temolae Keep, leaving their Gold behind to watch the house. Or at least that was the excuse they gave him, for leaving him behind after telling him they were spending the weekend at the castle.

When they arrived at the castle, Amber spent a bit of time with her mother and Jasper, who had arrived not long after she did, but was too restless to manage that for long. Flinn, Crystal, Morgan and Orin arrived well before lunch and Crystal talked excitedly about her plans for the rest of the year. Amber still wasn't certain that moving in with Flinn was the best choice for her friend, but didn't bother saying anything else. What could she say with the amount of time she spent with Ronan? He was far more hazardous to her health than Flinn could ever be to Crystal's.

Just before lunch Alsandair and Chait started to bring in more people using the excuse that they were joining them for the meal. All the secrecy was beginning to make Amber worry that they had a spy in their castle. When she said that directly to Kade, he laughed at her.

"Of course we do. Probably several. Just like we've got spies in the castles of some of our enemies. The trick is to figure out who the spies are so we can give them misinformation."

After that, Amber couldn't stop eyeing each of the servants that entered the dining room. It was crazy. Shouldn't they make sure all their staff was trustworthy? She looked around the table, her gaze resting first on her grandparents, sitting one on either side of her mother, Jasper across the table from them, and then on Roy and his family. Although it probably didn't matter since even their guests weren't all that trustworthy.

When lunch was over, they all headed for the planning room, after Amber had asked Gary to keep her mother distracted for a while. Before she reached the room, her grandparents cornered her.

"We want you to come back and train with the Knights," Charles said.

Amber stared at him for a few seconds hardly able to believe he'd said that. "You've got to be kidding."

"Stanley and Dominic have both been reprimanded. As will Wayne and Jennifer be when they're found."

"How? Were they made to jog around the track for an hour? Or maybe it was two hours." She didn't like the bitterness she could hear in her own voice. That wasn't her. None of this was her. Very soon she wouldn't be able to recognise herself.

Kade strode back towards them. "We're not about to let her go to your headquarters. We can't protect her there."

"This has nothing to do with you, dragon," Helen snarled.

Amber moved to stand beside Kade, her arm brushing against his. "Don't speak to Kade like that. And for the last time, I'm not interested in joining your Knights. All they think about is killing."

"And your dragons don't?" Charles demanded.

There was no answer she could give to that

question. Or at least none she wanted to give. "Why ask me? Why not Jay?"

"He wouldn't make a good Knight," Helen said.

Amber eyed her grandmother. Was that a compliment? "What makes you think I would?"

"You're not weak," Helen said.

Okay, that had to be a compliment. Especially coming from her grandmother. She shook her head. "I'm not interested. I've had enough of killing."

"Don't give me that rubbish. What do you think you're planning to do today? Stand back and watch the fight? Stop making idiotic comments," Helen said.

Obviously that was it for the compliments. Amber stared at her grandmother a moment longer. That warm and fuzzy moment certainly hadn't lasted long. "This conversation is over. Your Knights had their chance and they weren't interested in it." She spun, striding towards the planning room, Kade at her side.

He linked his fingers through hers, momentarily squeezing.

She looked up at him, smiling as she squeezed back. Her smile disappeared the moment she stepped into the planning room and saw that Ronan had arrived. It looked like she was about to find out what he had in mind. The dread she'd woken with returned with a vengeance.

Kade closed the door behind them, tugging Amber towards the table. She reluctantly followed, sitting down beside him.

Ronan's gaze went to Crystal. "Is the Void clear?"

Crystal nodded.

Ronan turned to Roy's family. "The moment Tahmid realises its a trap you need to get Roy out of there. That's the only reason I'm letting you join us. You're to kill only those that get in your way. Understand?"

Isaac and Eliza nodded, but Amos didn't bother to nod until Ronan turned his gaze directly on him.

"And what about us?" Charles asked. "You better not be expecting us to leave the moment the fighting starts."

Ronan smiled. "No, you may kill as many of their dragons as you want. Wasn't that the deal?" He held Charles' gaze a moment longer before he turned to Crystal again. "You already have your orders." When Crystal and Flinn nodded his gaze travelled the table, momentarily resting on Amber, Kade and Flinn. "None of your warriors will be able to be there without compromising the test. At least not in the Void. They can remain close and come in the moment the fight starts. They can bring Charles and Helen with them."

"We're not about to miss half the fight," Charles said.

"As if I'd leave Kade and Amber unprotected that long," Maira said.

"If we involve too many Golds, Kade and Flinn can't use it as a test," Ronan said.

Flinn gestured towards Roy's family. "We've already got three extra to bring Roy's family through the Void and one for Jasper. That's more than enough."

Amber thought she better cut in before an argument started and she missed out on hearing the plan for herself. "What do I need to do?"

Ronan's smile turned predatory. "What you do best, kitten." Holding her gaze he paused a moment. "Kill."

She fought against the urge to back away, holding onto the sides of her seat so she didn't move. "Kill who?"

"Tahmid."

Her grip tightened on the seat. "I would have thought you'd want to do that yourself."

"Either one of us, kitten. It's all the same. Aren't you mine?"

Amber opened her mouth to disagree, but Kade nudged her with his foot. She managed not to look in his direction. *"What?"*

"Don't throw his offer away, but don't acknowledge it directly either."

How did Kade expect her to do that? "So what do you want Kade and me to do? Get as close to Tahmid as possible?"

"That would probably be a good idea." Ronan rose from the table. "We should have just enough time for me to show you Golds the pathway through the Void to where Roy is to meet Tahmid."

"Where is it?" Amber asked.

"An abandoned industrial site a few hours from where Roy lives. We had to make it an area he'd be able to drive to. We don't want to make Tahmid suspicious." Ronan turned to Flinn. "You first."

Amber reached for Kade's hand. *"Be careful today."*

"Stop worrying."

She couldn't help it. There was no way she wanted to go through being told he was dead again. *"I've got a bad feeling about all of this. I think we need more warriors."*

"Everything will be fine. Or don't you believe I can protect you?"

Amber slowly smiled. Typical. *"Of course you can."*

She kept the rest of her thoughts to herself. *But it's you I'm worried about.*

Roy caught her gaze across the table. *"What's wrong?"*

"Nothing. I just don't like the waiting before a battle."

Roy nodded, turning to answer a question from his mother.

Chapter Twenty-Four

By the time Ronan had taken all the Golds through the Void and back again, Amber was pacing the room, sending a glare to her grandfather each time she passed him in his pacing.

Ronan spoke to Chait, Anrai and Alsandair. "Take the warriors and Knights to their waiting point." He gestured towards Helen and Charles. "Then take Roy to the car that's waiting for him. The rest of us will wait here for your return. Kade, time to let the Elders know the test location. They've had enough time to inform Tahmid that he was caught breaking the law and passing on information about the warrior tests and has lost his position."

Ronan's other gold, Turi, stood beside Jasper. Amber's gaze remained on Turi for several minutes. They needed to get Jasper a Gold that was loyal to them, not Ronan. She tried not to think about how

Jasper's last Gold had died. When Turi looked over in her direction, she held his gaze a moment longer before she went back to her pacing.

Chait returned from taking Roy to the car, causing Amber's stomach to do a slow turn. It was time. Kade stepped in front of her, halting her pacing, linking his fingers through hers.

"Ready?"

"I guess so." This time when Kade took her through the Void, they stayed in it. The world around them looked like it was covered by a light fog. She wondered how much harder it was to see through the Void in the dark. It was late afternoon now, hopefully they'd be out of the Void before they had a chance to find out. Holding Kade's hand tightly, she moved forward. The air was so heavy around them it was like walking underwater. "Where should we wait?"

"I don't know. I can't see Tahmid anywhere." He glanced over his shoulder. "But hopefully that's Roy driving up."

Amber turned to see a car drive through an open chain wire gate nearly two metres tall. The car stopped, the engine continuing to run for a minute before it was turned off. Roy climbed out of the car, closing the door behind him as he slowly walked forward, his gaze scanning the area. He walked straight towards them.

"What happens if he walks through us while we're in the Void?"

Kade chuckled. "It'll feel like a breeze passing through us."

"And what'll he feel?"

"I believe you humans have a saying about it. Someone just walked over my grave."

As Roy continued to come closer Amber tugged on Kade's hand, drawing him to the side. "I think that's an experience I can live without." She turned to watch Roy cross the pitted bitumen car park, headed towards the dilapidated building. "Where is Tahmid?"

"Maybe he's inside."

Amber followed behind Roy, slowly falling behind since it was harder to walk through the Void. "What happens if we need to get to him quickly?"

"We run. But whatever you do, don't let go of me."

She tightened her grip on his hand. "Do I really want to know why?"

"Probably not."

Roy stopped abruptly as Tahmid stepped out of the Void in front of him.

"If the information you have for me is worthless, your life will be too," Tahmid said.

"It isn't. Like I told you, it's about the mage. She almost got me killed when she escaped the Knights," Roy said.

"What makes you think I'm interested?"

Roy shrugged. "I heard everyone wants her, but you're the only dragon I know. You're my grandfather."

Tahmid laughed.

The sound sent a shiver through Amber. "And I thought Ronan was bad."

Still smiling, Tahmid said, "That means nothing to me, Knight. Hurry up and tell me what you know or you can take the information to the grave with you. I have more important things to deal with today. "

"I know where they've hidden her."

If Amber hadn't known that Ronan had asked Roy to do this, his behaviour would have convinced her he was about to betray her. A hand clasped hers and she started to scream, stopping when Crystal and Flinn appeared before her. "What are you doing? Give me heart failure, why don't you?"

Crystal grinned. "Sorry." Her grin faded. "I told–"

Amber swore, cutting Crystal off as she looked

around her. "We're surrounded. There must be fifty Golds in the Void."

"You can see them?" Crystal asked.

Amber nodded.

"I can too," Kade said.

"I wasn't sure you'd be able to. I thought it might only be dragons. But forget that."

"Forget the dragons?" Amber had no idea how she was meant to do that.

Crystal shook her head. "No, forget about how you can see them. I told Ronan how many there are, but he said to go ahead as planned. We can't kill that many before the dead bodies start appearing out of the Void," Crystal said.

Kade pointed to where three Golds stood near each other in the Void. "Head there. If we stay together we can take more out." He drew a dagger.

"We still won't take out enough." Flinn held a bloodstained dagger.

Kade walked towards the group. "We can try." He glanced at Amber. "Hold onto me so I've got two arms free."

Amber saw that Crystal had her fingers hooked into the waistband of Flinn's trousers so her fingers were pressed against his skin. She did the same to Kade, keeping hold of Crystal's hand so she could continue to see into the Void. When they reached the Golds, Amber looked away as Kade and Flinn grabbed hold of two, slitting their throats, holding onto them until they were dead, turning into dragons. They lowered them to the ground. As soon as they'd taken out the third one, they started moving towards another group of Golds.

Amber had trouble drawing her gaze away from the blood oozing from the dead dragons. Even blood didn't move properly in the Void. "This doesn't seem right."

"Of course it's right," Flinn said. "You use whatever advantage you've got."

"It seems like cheating. They can't see us." Amber looked away as they grabbed another two Golds.

"We'll still be outnumbered when we all come out of the Void to fight." Kade lowered the dragon to the ground.

"Yeah, but…" her voice trailed off as her gaze was again drawn to the blood that slowly oozed from the dragon on the ground. Did she want them to have a fighting chance? Wouldn't that put her friends and family at risk? She didn't know what to think anymore.

Flinn and Kade took out another four Golds before an alarm went on Crystal's phone. Her fingers momentarily tightened on Amber's. "Five minute warning before all hell breaks loose."

Amber looked towards Tahmid who was still questioning Roy. "I better get closer to Tahmid." Behind him she could see Ronan, near the wall of the building, his arms crossed as he watched everything.

"Good luck." Crystal let go of Amber's hand, disappearing.

"You too." She guessed Crystal heard her when her friend momentarily touched her arm, smiling before she disappeared again.

Kade took her hand from his waistband, walking towards Tahmid. "If we get behind Tahmid, we shouldn't be in the way of Roy's family when they try and get him out of here."

"I hope they get him away safely. There's a lot of Golds that'll be attacking us."

"Don't worry about them. Focus on taking out Tahmid. We have to get to him before he leaves through the Void. This will be our only chance. He'll be on his guard after this and we'll need several armies to take him down."

For a moment Amber wished Kade hadn't told her that. She didn't want to remember what it looked like to attack with an army, but then she was glad.

It hadn't occurred to her he might run. She'd been expecting him to stay and fight. "Okay."

"Remember, it's survival of the fittest."

With the amount of times she'd been told, it wasn't likely she'd forget. She kept the words to herself, nodding instead. They stopped close behind Tahmid who was telling Roy to hurry up and explain himself properly. Amber smiled at how well Roy was doing with his garbled explanation.

A Gold stepped out of the Void. "Tahmid!" He pointed towards two dragons lying dead on the ground.

Tahmid reached for Roy. His family, and the Golds with them, came out of the Void, pulling Roy away from him.

When Kade brought them out of the Void, Amber let go of him, drawing her daggers. Tahmid spun to face her so that she met his gaze as she drove the daggers into him, her arms wrapped around his body. Shock filled his eyes as he dragged them into the Void. Amber saw Golds pouring out of the Void to attack her allies, but she couldn't let Tahmid go. He took her with him through the Void, struggling to break her grip as he came out in a large bedroom with stone walls and a carpeted floor.

Tahmid finally broke free and Amber stumbled

backwards. She threw herself at him, sinking one of the blades into his arm as he tried to draw his sword. Around her she sensed people moving rapidly towards the room they were in and guessed Tahmid had called his warriors to help him. She didn't have long.

Again Tahmid broke free from her and this time when Amber sprang at him, she dropped her daggers. Turning into a panther, she pinned him to the ground, going for his throat. Before she managed to tear into him, he twisted under her, becoming a dragon. Then he was above her, flames pouring from his mouth. She turned human, one of her hands reaching for a dagger as she rolled out of the way of the flames. Calling up her own flames, she plunged her fiery dagger into the dragon, forcing it between two scales, her hand coated with blood as she pressed deeper.

He roared, rearing back before he dropped down to strike at her. Blood stained the carpet as she threw herself out of the way, jumping to her feet to draw her sword. It burst into flames as she spun, driving it into Tahmid as the bedroom door burst open. Blood coated her arm and, letting go of her sword, she leapt out of the way as Tahmid collapsed onto his side. She heard his heartbeat slow, blood continuing to flow from him.

In the doorway stood five warriors, swords drawn as they tried to crowd into the room. None of them attacked. They continued to stand there, staring at her.

She didn't know what to do. Where was Ronan when she needed him? Mentally searching for him didn't help. He must still be in her world because she couldn't find him. She took a step backwards, running into the dead dragon. Trying to recall what the room looked like behind her, she continued to warily watch the warriors. Amber couldn't even remember if there was an open window. She certainly couldn't fly past the warriors in the doorway. Not without being cut down. What were they waiting for? Her phone started to ring, but she ignored it. Now wasn't the time for taking calls.

The warriors in the doorway parted and a single warrior stood there, sword drawn and pointed at Amber. "You will pay with your life for the one you stole."

If the man hadn't been so serious, she would have rolled her eyes at his theatrical comment. Raising her hands, she formed fireballs. "I don't think you really want to do that." Her phone stopped ringing and she was glad it didn't start again.

The man stepped into the room. The warriors closed ranks behind him. "You killed my father. I'm going to rip your heart out and eat it."

Oh crap. For a moment she thought she'd spoken the words aloud. A small measure of relief filled her when she realised she hadn't. Never show weakness. She smiled, trying to mimic Ronan's predatory one. "I'm sure you think you'll manage that, but you won't live long enough to do it."

The man laughed. "I know mages. We still have one here. You are pathetic, weak creatures. My father was probably already mortally wounded by your warrior before he came home with you."

She thought of Cooper. Yeah, if he'd been the only mage she'd known then she'd think the same as this man. Hopefully he was about to learn differently. She really didn't want to die. "The only wounds Tahmid suffered today were the ones I gave him." She could see his son didn't believe her.

The man gestured towards the sword embedded in his father. "Take your weapon. I will avenge him with honour."

Amber started to move, then froze as she felt Ronan in the distance. He was somewhere in the dragon lands, but not close enough for her to mentally contact him. Then he was gone and when he came back into the world again he was even further away.

"Now."

The man's word snapped her back to the room and she picked up the dagger lying on the floor before she pulled the one from Tahmid's body.

"Leave them. Your sword, mage. Fight me like a warrior, not an assassin."

She slid the blades into her wrist sheaths, hoping she'd actually get a chance to clean the blood from them later. No matter how distasteful a chore it would be. Was that what Ronan was trying to turn her into? An assassin? Struggling to draw the sword from Tahmid's body she again felt Ronan flash in and out of the world. He was going in the wrong direction. The sword free, she faced Tahmid's son. Fighting the urge to ask him his name, she raised her sword. She would have no choice but to kill him. Having his name wouldn't make it any easier.

"Pathetic. You don't even know how to hold your sword correctly."

Her chin rose and she met his gaze squarely. "And yet I was still able to kill your father. What does that say about him?"

"That you got lucky."

Maybe she could keep him talking long enough that she'd figure a way out of here. Ronan now seemed to be coming closer to her with every flash in and out of the world. "No, I think the phrase you're looking for is that he was beyond pathetic."

The man came closer and Amber moved away from Tahmid. She didn't want to risk tripping over his body during the fight. Trying to keep an eye on the man in front of her while she assessed possible exits was nearly impossible. Catching a glimpse of a closed window, she jumped to the side as the man attacked. There was no way she could beat him in a sword fight. As he came at her again, she sheathed her sword, turning into a goshawk and shooting past him to land on the other side of the room, as a human. Her scan of the room had shown her two windows with closed wooden shutters. Things didn't look good.

"Stand and fight me, mage." He attacked again and once more Amber avoided him by turning into a goshawk.

Becoming human, she grinned at him. "Having a little trouble catching me, are you?" If she drew him across the room maybe she could fly back over and get one of the windows open before he could reach her.

"Pathetic." Sword swinging, he attacked, nearly getting her.

Before Amber could work out how the window was locked, she felt Ronan close enough to send her thoughts to him. *"Ronan."* She landed, warily watching the man who had turned to face her.

"Where are you?"

"I'm guessing in a castle."

"Where's Tahmid?"

"Dead."

"If you don't stand and fight me, I'll make you suffer," the man warned at the same time as Ronan spoke.

"What were you thinking, going with him like that?"

She thought it was probably best not to tell him she hadn't planned to go with Tahmid. *"He was getting away."*

"I knew you could kill him, kitten."

"Yeah well, his son is trying very hard to make that my last kill." Her contact with Ronan disappeared and then she felt him closer. *"You're headed in the right direction. You're much closer now."* She slowly walked to the side, her gaze not leaving the man.

"He headed for his main castle. Get out of there, Amber.

Four of his sons are in residence. It'd be suicide coming in there after you."

Chapter Twenty-Five

Amber's heart sank. She'd thought Ronan would be able to help her. He obviously didn't think she stood a chance if he was calling her by her name. *"The windows are shut and I'm a little busy trying not to get killed to open them."* Launching a fireball at the man, she leapt into the air as a goshawk, streaking across the room to land on the window ledge, staying in bird form.

"Where in the castle are you?" Ronan was coming closer.

Amber watched the man, waiting until the last moment to fly out of his way. The sword struck the window, but it remained closed. *"A bedroom."* She landed on the other window ledge.

"Try and be helpful, kitten."

It was a relief to hear him call her that. Maybe she'd manage to survive after all. Again she flew out of the way at the last minute. The man roared as he spun to face her. *"That's as helpful as I can be. Stone walls, carpet and a timber bed. A bedroom."* Ronan was even closer now, maybe only minutes away.

The man launched himself at her and Amber felt his blade sweep past her as she flew to the other window. The sound of steel on timber sounded behind her.

"What shaped windows are they?"

Dodging another attack, Amber tried to focus on not getting killed. She didn't know how much longer she could last before he got lucky with his wild swings. *"Arched."* She screeched, glad she wasn't human so that the laughter drawn from her wasn't obvious. She couldn't help thinking about having watched Playschool when she was younger. It looked like today she needed to be able to see through the arched window.

"Stay still!" The man's attacks were growing wilder. Chips of timber flew into the room each time he hit the shutters.

As if she was about to make his job any easier by standing still for him. She sensed another person headed towards them. Was it another son? Two vengeful dragons might be more than even she could handle.

"Get one of them open," Ronan ordered.

For a moment she was confused until she remembered they'd been talking about the windows. It was a little hard to focus on anything other than the dragon who wanted her dead and was putting in a lot of effort to achieve his goal. But what choice did she have? *"I'll see what I can do."*

"Hurry up before someone spots me."

The man attacked her again, this time his sword clashing with the stone window frame. She was halfway across the room when another man burst into the room, fireballs in his hands.

"Attack her." The man ordered. "But stay out of the way. This room isn't big enough for three to fight in."

Amber dodged behind the man and the fireballs barely missed both of them.

"What do you think you're doing?" The man pointed his sword in the direction of his mage.

"You told me to attack her."

Amber screeched, amusement cutting through her fear. She reached for the mind of the other mage and was surprised she was able to communicate with him so easily. *"We have Cooper. He's free."*

The mage looked in her direction. *"Prove it."*

She tried to think of a way to prove it, but drew a

blank for a moment. *"He likes to draw fantasy art on a computer tablet."*

"He's safe?"

"Usually, but he is free and we protect him." She flew out of the reach of the sword that came for her.

"Will you protect me?" He launched an attack at her. It went wide. *"Sorry. I have to make it look good."*

"All I can promise is to try and get you away from here." She reached for Ronan's mind. *"If I can get a mage to jump out the window, can you catch him?"*

"If I know what window it is."

"You're very close. No, other direction. Yes, keep on that course and you'll be at the window." She dodged another halfhearted attack from the mage and a more serious one from Tahmid's son. Speaking to the mage, she said, *"I'll fly past the windows, launch fireballs at them. We need to get one open. If you jump out, my dragon will catch you."* She wheeled around and flew past the window. The sound of splintering timber rang out behind her, followed by the clash of steel and stone.

"Jumping out a window to possible death can't be worse than living here," the mage said.

"Was that you, kitten?"

"What?"

"The fireball coming out the window."

"*No. It was the mage I want you to catch.*"

"*Tell him to jump. I'm ready.*"

"*If anything happens to him, Ronan…*" she let the sentence trail off.

"*Hurry up. I can see movement,*" Ronan ordered.

"*Are there any other mages?*" Amber asked the mage.

"*No. They'd planned to capture you before they made more. We weren't good enough for them. They wanted to know how to make us properly.*"

"*Then get out the window. Ronan will catch you.*"

"*Do you promise?*"

"*Yes. Now go before it's too late.*" She felt the brush of steel. A piece of feather drifted to the floor. "*Now!*"

The mage ran across the room, throwing himself out the window.

"Elliot! Get back here." The man dashed to the window, hanging out it. He bellowed in rage. "Ronan!"

Amber shot through the small gap above the man's head, arrowing through the sky towards Ronan who clutched Elliot in his front claws. "*Where is everyone?*" She made sure both Ronan and Elliot could hear her.

"*At Kade's place.*"

"*In the human world?*"

"*Yes.*"

"They're all safe?"

"They were when I left them."

"Take Elliot to Cooper then come back for me. You can take me to Kade. I'll keep flying in this direction."

Ronan didn't bother answering. Instead he disappeared into the Void. She felt him come out of it, a long way from her and guessed that was where Temolae Keep was. Fighting the urge to turn in the direction of her castle, she reminded herself that Ronan wouldn't be able to find her if she changed directions. Then Ronan came out of the Void behind her. Not far behind him she sensed other dragons giving chase. She wheeled around, aiming for Ronan. His claws closed over her and she was taken through the Void to Ronan's home. As soon as he let her go, she turned human, glancing towards the water garden, visible in the grey light filling the sky. It was nearly dawn. How had an entire night passed? No wonder she was exhausted.

Ronan landed beside her, also becoming human. He eyed her up and down. "Any of that your blood?"

She shook her head, anger coursing through her. She was getting sick of this place.

"Are you certain Tahmid is dead?"

She nodded. And sick of being dragged wherever Ronan wanted her to go.

"Have you forgotten how to speak, kitten?"

She shook her head, gaining control of her anger. "I was just trying to figure out if you were getting deaf in your old age. Or maybe you've lost your ability to find your way through the pathways of the Void. This doesn't look anything like Kade's place."

"In case you're interested, Roy and his family made it out safely. They should be back at their own home by now."

"I am interested, but you didn't need to bring me here to tell me this."

"I delivered Elliot to Cooper. Flinn took his warriors and Crystal back to his place and they're all unharmed."

"What do you really want, Ronan?" A hand started to go to her hip then she dropped it when she remembered all the blood on it.

"You at my side when I take the Council seat in a couple of hours."

She shook her head. "That wasn't part of the deal. Not really. All I had to do was help you-" she hesitated, unable to bring herself to say kill. "Deal with Tahmid."

Ronan closed the small distance that was between them. "I know you, kitten. You were born for this."

He reached out and lifted her hand, turning it so her dagger was visible.

Amber tugged her hand from his grip. "For what? An assassin? Not likely. Now take me to Kade's."

Ronan smiled, all predator, gold in the depths of his blue eyes. "No. Not an assassin. You don't have it in you to sneak around in the shadows. A Dragon Mage. A warrior." He took hold of her hand, taking her through the Void.

When they came out into Kade's lounge room everyone was shouting. Charles and Helen both had their swords drawn, facing Kade who had his hand on the hilt of his while Jasper was trying to tell Charles and Helen to put their weapons away.

"Enough!" Amber shouted.

The room was filled with silence for a split second before everyone started talking at once. Ronan leaned back against the wall near the front door, a smile of amusement. Amber shook her head. This was ridiculous. Hadn't they just fought together against an enemy? And yet still they fought amongst themselves.

She stepped between Charles and Kade, her gaze on Charles. "Stop it. I won't let you hurt him."

"She doesn't belong to you Knights," Ronan said.

Amber rounded on Ronan, about to say she didn't belong to him.

Kade spoke before she could. "Do you want to go somewhere quieter?"

She was sick of always having to watch what she said. Sick of the fights. Her gaze was drawn to the blood on her hands. Sick of battle and sick of the blood. Always there was blood. Even in her dreams.

Helen pointed a finger at Kade. "Stay away from her. If it wasn't for you, she'd be a Knight."

"If it wasn't for Kade, Grandad would still be imprisoned." She shouted the words, trying not to, but it was impossible. She was so tired. Tired of everything. She just wanted her life back. And this wasn't it. Again her gaze was drawn to the blood on her hands. It was nothing like her life.

"I would have escaped eventually," Charles said.

He had to disagree with everything. Her gaze roamed the room, before being drawn back to her bloodstained hands. "I can't do this anymore." She headed for the front door.

"Where are you going?" Helen demanded.

She stopped, still facing the door. She didn't have a clue. Where could she go? Turning, she faced Helen. "I'll stay at your place until school finishes and then I'm gone. It's not like you're using it."

"What do you mean, gone?" Kade crossed the room, reaching for her.

She sidestepped him. "I can't do this anymore. It's not me." She held up her hands. "Look at them. Ten. I've killed ten people." A sharp laugh burst from her. "I can count them on my two hands. How long before that's no longer possible? How long before I lose count?"

"Amber-"

Again she stepped away from Kade. "I just can't. I need to get away from all this mess." She couldn't meet his gaze. The words were hard enough to speak. If she looked into his eyes she knew she wouldn't be able to say them.

"What about Topaz?" Jasper asked. "She has to go back Tuesday."

It took her a moment before she could think what to do. "I'll go with Ronan Tuesday and tell them you will make the exchange in future." She started to turn away.

"I always knew you were weak," Helen spat the words.

She met her grandmother's gaze, anger pushing the pain away. Anger. She was sick of anger. That wasn't her. The blood, the anger, the fear. She didn't have a clue who she was these days, but that wasn't her.

Words began to form, but she changed her mind. Her grandmother's comment didn't deserve acknowledging. As she turned to the door, she caught Ronan's gaze, a slight smile of amusement on his lips. She pointed a bloodstained finger at him. "And you stay out of my life."

Ronan chuckled. *"You know my number, kitten."* He vanished into the Void.

He was wrong. She was done. She strode outside, staring at the road. It was a long way to town and she wasn't about to walk it. She'd have to fly. A panther would cause too much unwanted attention.

"Amber!"

She kept walking, trying to ignore how the tone of Kade's voice cut into her.

He ran after her, stepping in front of her. "Don't go." His voice was soft, his words a plea.

She shook her head. "I can't do this anymore. I have to go." Could hearts break? Is that what the ache in her chest was?

"Please."

She almost gave in. Closing her eyes she took a deep breath. Her lungs filled with the scent of him. Dragon. Forcing herself to meet his gaze, she said. "I can't stay. If I do-" she broke off, looking to the side.

Kade reached for her, but she backed away. His

hand curled into a fist as it dropped to his side. "Don't do this. How can you even think about leaving? You say you love me. If you did, you couldn't walk away. It would be ripping you apart."

"It's ripping me apart to stay." She swallowed, finding it almost impossible. "It's turning me into someone I'm not." The blood was drying on her hands. How long would it take to remove those stains?

"Wait until the end of the year and I'll go with you."

She shook her head. "Don't you see? You'll still be a Gold Warrior. I can't be a part of that." Her eyes burned as she held his gaze a moment more before she stepped around him and kept on walking, images of blood filling the world around her. It looked like she'd have to walk. There was no way she could change form without the panther forcing her way out. And if she was going to do this, if she was going to take her life back, she needed to leave it all behind. The fire, the goshawk, the panther and most of all the dragons. Her eyes momentarily closed. The dragons. A dragon. That was the hardest part of all. But this wasn't her. She needed to figure out who she was before she became someone she wasn't.

Free Ebook

Subscribe to Avril's newsletter and receive a free ebook. This ebook is exclusive to those on her mailing list. To find out more about this offer visit:

www.avrilsabine.com/free-ebook

*

We value your privacy and will not sell, rent, exchange or loan your email address to third parties. Your information is confidential and you are under no obligation to remain on the mailing list and can unsubscribe at any time.

Acknowledgements

As always, thanks to the usual crew. I dread to think how many mistakes there'd be without you.

To The Reader

If you enjoyed this book, why not consider leaving a review to help other readers discover it too? Reader engagement is one of the few ways that lets an author know readers want more books in a particular series or genre. So leave a review and tell friends, not only about this book but also about other ones you've enjoyed, so you can continue to enjoy books by your favourite authors for years to come.

Dreams are meant to be lived,

Avril.

About The Author

Avril is an Australian author who lives with her family on acreage in South East Queensland. She writes mostly young adult and children's speculative fiction, but has been known to dabble in other genres. You can find more information about her at www.avrilsabine.com where you can also subscribe to her newsletter to be kept informed about new releases, current projects, blog posts and exclusive news.

Titles By Avril Sabine

Stories about strong characters and characters who discover their strengths.

SERIES

Assassins Of The Dead- Young Adult Fantasy/ Paranormal

Book 1: Dark Blade

Book 2: Dragon Touched

Book 3: Society Against Vampires

Book 4: King's Request

Dragon Blood- Young Adult Urban Fantasy (with elements of romance)

(5 book series)

Book 1: Pliethin

Book 2: Wyvern

Book 3: Surety

Book 4: Knight

Book 5: Mage

Dragon Mage- Young Adult Urban Fantasy (with elements of romance)

(Series two of Dragon Blood series)

Book 1: Promise

Dragon Blood Chronicles- Young Adult Urban Fantasy (with elements of romance)

(Companion stand alone series to Dragon Blood)

Book 1: Oath

Book 2: Betrayed

Guardians Of The Round Table- Young Adult Fantasy LitRPG

(Co-written with Storm and Rhys Petersen)

Book 1: Dexterity Fail

Book 2: Goblin Boots

Book 3: Singed Feathers

Book 4: Frog Mage

Book 5: Crystal Mine

Book 6: Cursed Harp

Rosie's Rangers- Young Adult Western Steampunk

(6 book series)

Book 1: Justice

Book 2: Vengeance

Book 3: Treachery

Book 4: Accused

Book 5: Wanted

Book 6: Corruption

Mark Of Kings- Children's Fantasy

(Upper middle grade/preteen)

(4 book series)

Book 1: The Arena

Book 2: The Island

Book 3: The Assassin

Book 4: The King

STAND ALONE SERIES

Demon Hunters- Young Adult Urban Fantasy/ Horror (with elements of romance)

Book 1: Blood Sacrifice

Book 2: Retribution

Book 3: Tainted

Book 4: Premonition

Book 5: Cursed

Book 6: Feud

Book 7: Extrication

Plea Of The Damned- Young Adult Urban Fantasy/Paranormal

(6 book series)

Book 1: Forgive Me Lucy

Book 2: Forgive Me Aiden

Book 3: Forgive Me Jena

Book 4: Forgive Me Kobe

Book 5: Forgive Me Marti

Book 6: Forgive Me Dawson

Realms Of The Fae- Young Adult Urban Fantasy (with elements of romance)

The Sword (short story in Like A Girl Anthology)

Heart Of Stone

Book 1: A Debt Owed

Book 2: Marked By The Hunt

Book 3: The Magic Collector

Book 4: An Unexpected Betrayal

Book 5: Imprisoned By Iron

Fairytales Retold (Short Stories)

Snow-White And Rose-Red

The Twelve Brothers

The Light Princess

Beauty And The Beast

Sleeping Beauty

Aschenputtel

The Golden Bird

The Frog Prince

The Death Of Koshchei The Deathless

Myths And Legends Retold (Short Stories)

Ion, Son Of Apollo

Sir Gawain And The Maid With The Narrow Sleeves

Princess Ilse, The Giant's Daughter

YOUNG ADULT NOVELS

Young Adult Fantasy (with elements of romance)

Elf Sight

Earth Bound

Young Adult Urban Fantasy

Stone Warrior (with elements of romance)

The Jungle Inside

Young Adult Contemporary (with elements of romance)

Through Your Eyes

The Ugly Stepsister

Perfect Little Princess

Young Adult Contemporary/Paranormal

Whispers In The Dark (with elements of romance and same sex relationships)

Over Too Soon (with elements of romance)

Young Adult Sci-Fi

Experiment X-One-Six (Urban Sci-Fi/Superheroes)

An Endless Dawn (Post Apocalyptic Sci-Fi)

CHILDREN'S BOOKS

Dragon Lord (Preteen/early teens) (Fantasy)

The Irish Wizard (Upper middle grade) (Urban Fantasy)

SHORT STORIES

Urban Fantasy

Eternally Late

Dealings With Joe

Glimpses (short story in That Moment When Anthology)

Contemporary

The Brat Next Door

Fantasy LitRPG

(Set in the same world as Guardians Of The Round Table Series)

Tales Of Inadon 1: The Disc (Co-written with Storm and Rhys Petersen) (short story in Game On! Anthology)

Post Apocalyptic Sci-Fi

Compulsive Directive

NONFICTION

A Year Of Weekly Writing Exercises (Creative Writing)

Cooking For Families With Allergies (Cooking) (Co-written with Storm Petersen)

Tell Me A Story, Grandma (Memoir)

For the most up to date details on available titles visit:

www.avrilsabine.com/books/bibliography

Dragon Blood Series

To learn more about this series visit:

www.avrilsabine.com/series/db

BOOKS AVAILABLE IN THE DRAGON BLOOD SERIES

(5 book series)

Book 1: Pliethin

Book 2: Wyvern

Book 3: Surety

Book 4: Knight

Book 5: Mage

BOOKS SET IN THE SAME WORLD AS THE DRAGON BLOOD SERIES

Dragon Mage- Young Adult Urban Fantasy (with elements of romance)

(Series two of Dragon Blood series)

Book 1: Promise

Dragon Blood Chronicles- Young Adult Urban Fantasy (with elements of romance)

(Companion stand alone series to Dragon Blood)

Book 1: Oath

Book 2: Betrayed

Disclaimer

This is a work of fiction. Names, characters, businesses, places, events and incidents are either the products of the author's imagination or used in a fictitious manner. Any resemblance to actual persons, living or dead, or actual events is purely coincidental. The opinions expressed or beliefs held are those of the characters and should not be assumed to be the opinions or beliefs of the author.